WUNPOST

**Center Point
Large Print**

**This Large Print Book carries the
Seal of Approval of N.A.V.H.**

WUNPOST

Dane Coolidge

CENTER POINT LARGE PRINT
THORNDIKE, MAINE

This Center Point Large Print edition
is published in the year 2012 by arrangement with
Golden West Literary Agency.

First published in the US by E.P. Dutton & Company.
First published in the UK by Hodder and Stoughton.

The text of this Large Print edition is unabridged.
In other aspects, this book may vary
from the original edition.
Printed in the United States of America
on permanent paper.
Set in 16-point Times New Roman type.

ISBN: 978-1-61173-335-8

Library of Congress Cataloging-in-Publication Data

Coolidge, Dane, 1873–1940.
Wunpost / Dane Coolidge. — Large print ed.
p. cm. — (Center Point large print edition)
ISBN 978-1-61173-335-8 (library binding : alk. paper)
1. Large type books. I. Title.
PS3505.O5697W96 2012
813′.52—dc23

2011046828

CONTENTS

WUNPOST

CHAPTER I

THE DEATH VALLEY TRAIL

THE heat hung like smoke above Panamint Sink, it surged up against the hills like the waves of a great sea that boiled and seethed in the sun; and the mountains that walled it in gleamed and glistened like polished jet where the light was struck back from their sides. They rose up in solid ramparts, unbelievably steep and combed clean by the sluicings of cloudbursts; and where the black canyons had belched forth their floods a broad wash spread out, writhing and twisting like a snake-track, until at last it was lost in the Sink. For the Sink was the swallower-up of all that came from the hills and whatever it sucked in it buried beneath its sands or poisoned on its alkali flats. Yet the Death Valley trail led across its level floor—thirty miles from Wild Rose Springs to Blackwater and its saloons—and while the heat danced and quivered there was a dust in the north pass and a pack-train swung round the point.

It came on furiously, four burros with flat packs and an old man who ran cursing behind; and as he passed down into the Sink there was another dust in the north and a lone man followed as furiously after him. He was young

9

and tall, a mountain of rude strength, and as he strode off down the trail he brandished a piece of quartz and swung his hat in the air. But the pack-train kept on, a column of swirling dust, a blotch of burro-gray in the heat; and as he emptied his canteen he hurled it to the ground and took after his partner on the run. He could see the twinkling feet, the heave of the white packs, the vindictive form dodging behind; and then his knees weakened, his throbbing brain seemed to burst and he fell down cursing in the trail. But the pack-train went on like a tireless automaton that no human power could stay and when he raised his head it was a streamer of dust, a speck on the far horizon.

He rose up slowly and looked around—at the empty trail, the waterless flats, the barren hills all about—and then he raised his fist, which still clutched the chunk of quartz, and shook it at the pillar of dust. His throat was dry and no words came, to carry the burden of his hate, but as he stumbled along his eyes were on the dust-cloud and he choked out gusty oaths. A demoniac strength took possession of his limbs and once more he broke into a run, the muttered oaths grew louder and gave way to savage shouts and then to delirious babblings; and when he awoke he was groveling in a sand-wash and the sun had sunk in the west.

Once more he rose up and looked down the

empty trail and across the waterless flats; and then he raised his eyes to the eastern hills, burning red in the last rays of the sun. They were high, very high, with pines on their summits, and from the wash of a near canyon there lapped out a tongue of green, the promise of water beyond. But his strength had left him now and given place to a feverish weakness—the hills were far away, and he could only sit and wait, and if help did not come he would perish. The solemn twilight turned to night, a star glowed in the east; and then, on the high point above the mouth of the canyon, there leapt up a brighter glow. It was a fire, and as he gazed he saw a form passing before it and feeding the ruddy blaze. He rose up all atremble, crushed down a brittle salt-bush and touched it off with a match; and as the resinous wood flared up he snatched out a torch and carried the flame to another bush. It was the signal of the lost, two fires side by side, and he gave a hoarse cry when, from the point of the canyon, a second fire promised help. Then he sank down in the sand, feebly feeding his signal fire, until he was roused by galloping feet.

A half moon was in the sky, lighting the desert with ghostly radiance, and as he scrambled up to look he saw a boy on a white mule, riding in with a canteen held out. Not a word was spoken but as he gurgled down the water he rolled his eyes and gazed at his rescuer. The boy was slim and

11

vigorous, stripped down to sandals and bib-overalls; and conspicuously on his hip he carried a heavy pistol which he suddenly hitched to the front.

"That's enough, now," he said, "you give me back that canteen." And when the man refused he snatched it from his lips and whipped out his ready gun. "Don't you grab me," he warned, "or I'll fill you full of lead. You've had enough, I tell you!"

For a moment the man faced him as if crouching for a spring; and then his legs failed him and he sank to the ground, at which the boy dropped down and stooped over him.

"Lie still," he said, "and I'll bathe your face— I was afraid you were crazy with the heat."

"That's all right, kid," muttered the man, "you're right on the job. Say, gimme another drink."

"In a minute—well, just a little one! Now, lie down here in the sand and try to go to sleep." He moistened a big handkerchief and sopped water on his head and over his heaving chest, and after a few drinks the big frame relaxed and the man lay sleeping like a child. But in his dreams he was still lost and running across the desert, he started and twitched his arms; and then he began to mutter and fumble in the sand until at last he sat up with a jerk.

"Where's that rock?" he demanded. "By grab,

12

she's half gold—I'm going to take it and bash out his brains!" He rose to his knees and scrambled about and the boy dropped his hand to his gun. "I'm going to *kill* him!" raved the man, "the danged old lizard-herder—he went off and left me to die!"

He felt about in the dirt and grabbed up the chunk of quartz, which he had lost in his last delirium.

"Look at *that!*" he exclaimed thrusting it out to the boy, "the richest danged quartz in the world! I've got a ledge of it, kid, enough to make us both rich—and John Calhoun never forgets a friend! No, and he never forgets an enemy—the son of a goat don't live that can put one over on *me!* You just wait, Mister Dusty Rhodes!"

"Oh, was that Dusty Rhodes?" the boy piped up eagerly. "I was watching from the point and I *thought* it was his outfit—but I don't think I've ever seen you. Were you glad when you saw my fire?"

"You bet I was, kid," the man answered gravely, "I reckon you saved my life. My name is John C. Calhoun."

He held out his hand and after a moment's hesitation the boy reached out and took it.

"My name is Billy Campbell and we live in Jail Canyon. My mother will be coming down soon—that is, if she can catch our other mule."

13

"Glad to meet her," replied Calhoun still shaking his hand, "you're a good kid, Billy; I like you. And when your mother comes, if it's agreeable to her, I'd like to take you along for my pardner. How would that suit you, now—I've just made a big strike and I'll put you right next to the discovery."

"I—I'd like it," stammered the boy hastily drawing his hand away, "only—only I'm afraid my mother won't let me. You see the boys are all gone, and there's lots of work to do, and—but I do get awful lonely."

"I'll fix it!" announced Calhoun, pausing to take another drink, "and anything I've got, it's yours. You've saved my life, Billy, and I never forget a kindness—any more than I forget an injury. Do you see that rock?" he demanded fiercely. "I'm going to follow Dusty Rhodes to the end of the world and bash out his rabbit brains with it! I stopped up at Black Point to look at that big dyke and what do you think he done? He went off and *left* me and never looked back until he struck them Blackwater saloons! And the first chunk of rock that I knocked off of that ledge would assay a thousand dollars—gold! I ran after that danged fool until I fell down like I was dead, and then I ran after him again, but he never so much as looked back—and all the time I was trying to make him rich and put him next to my strike!"

He stopped and mopped his brow, then took another drink and laughed, deep down in his chest.

"We were supposed to be prospecting," he said at last. "I threw in with him over at Furnace Creek and we never stopped hiking until we struck the upper water at Wild Rose. How's that for prospecting—never looked at a rock, except them he threw at his burros—and this morning, when I stopped, he got all bowed up and went off and left me flat. All I had was one canteen and the makings for a smoke, everything else was on the jacks, and the first rock I knocked off was rotten with gold—he'd been going past it for years! Well, I *stopped!* Nothing to it, when you find a ledge like that you want to put up a notice. All my blanks were in the pack but I located it, all the same—with some rocks and a cigarette paper. It'll hold, all right, according to law—it's got my name, and the date, and the name of the claim and how far I claim, both ways—but not a doggoned corner nor a pick-mark on it; and there it is, right by the trail! The first jasper that comes by is going to jump it, sure—don't you know, boy, I've got to get *back.* What's the chances for borrowing your mule?"

"What—Tellurium?" faltered the boy going over to the mule and rubbing his nose regretfully, "he's—he's a pet; I'd rather not."

"Aw come on now, I'll pay you well—I'll stake

15

you the claim next to mine. That ought to be worth lots of money."

"Nope," returned Billy, "here's a lunch I brought along. I guess I'll be going home."

He untied a sack of food from the back of his saddle and mounted as if to go, but the stranger took the mule by the bit.

"Now listen, kid," he said. "Do you know who I am? Well, I'm John C. Calhoun, the man that discovered the Wunpost Mine and put Southern Nevada on the map. I'm no crazy man; I'm a prospector, as good as the best, if I am playing to a little hard luck. Yes sir, I located the Wunpost and started that first big rush—they came pouring into Keno by the thousands; but when I show 'em this rock there won't be anybody left—they'll come across Death Valley like a sandstorm. They'll come pouring down that wash like a cloudburst in July and the whole doggoned country will be located. Don't you want to be in on the strike? I'm giving you a chance, and you'll never have another one like it. All I ask is this mule, and your canteen and the grub, and I'll tell you what I'll do—I'll give you half my claim, and I'll bet it's worth millions, and I'll bring back your mule to boot!"

"Oh, will you?" exclaimed the boy and was scrambling swiftly down when he stopped with one hand on the horn. "Does—does it make any difference if I'm a girl?" he asked with a break in

16

his voice, and John C. Calhoun started back. He looked again and in the desert moonlight the boyish face seemed to soften and change. Tears sprang into the dark eyes and as she hung her head a curl fell across her breast.

"Hell—no!" he burst out hardly knowing what he said, "not as long as I get the mule."

"Then write out that notice for Wilhelmina Campbell—I guess that's my legal name."

"It's a right pretty name," conceded Calhoun as he mounted, "but somehow I kinder liked Billy."

CHAPTER II

THE GATEWAY OF DREAMS

STANDING alone in the desert, with her face bared to the moonlight and her curls shaken free to the wind, Wilhelmina smiled softly as she gazed after the stranger who already had won her heart. His language had been crude when he thought she was a boy, but that only proved the perfection of her disguise; and when she had asked if it made any difference, and confessed that she was a girl, he had bridged over the gap like a flash. "Hell—no!" he had said, as men oftentimes do to express the heartiest accord; and then he had added, with the gallantry due a lady, that Wilhelmina was a right pretty name. And tomorrow, as soon as he had staked out his claim—their claim—he was coming back to the ranch!

She started back up the long wash that led down from Jail Canyon, still musing on his masterful ways, but as she rounded the lower point and saw a light in the house a sudden doubt assailed her. Tellurium was her mule, to give to whom she chose, but he was matched to pull with Bodie when they needed a team and her father might not approve. And what would she say when she met her mother's eye and she

18

questioned her about this strange man? Yet she knew as well as anything that he was going to make her rich—and tomorrow he would bring back the mule. All she needed was faith, and the patience to wait; and she took her scolding so meekly that her mother repented it and allowed her to sleep in the tunnel.

The Jail Canyon Ranch lay in a pocket among the hills, so shut in by high ridges and overhanging rimrock that it seemed like the bottom of a well; but where the point swung in that encircled the tiny farm a tunnel bored its way through the hill. It was the extension of a mine which in earlier days had gophered along the hillside after gold, but now that it was closed down and abandoned to the rats Wilhelmina had taken the tunnel for her own. It ran through the knife-blade ridge as straight as a die, and a trail led up to its mouth; and from the other side, where it broke out into the sun, there was a view of the outer world. Sitting within its cool portal she could look off across the Sink, to Blackwater and the Argus Range beyond; and by stepping outside she could see the whole valley, from South Pass to the Death Valley Trail.

It was from this tunnel that she had watched when Dusty Rhodes went past, a moving fleck of color plumed with dust; and when the sun sank low she had seen the form that followed, like a man yet not like a man. She had seen it rise and fall, disappear and loom up again; until at last in the twilight she had challenged it with a fire and the answer had led her to—him. She had found him—lost on the desert and about to die, big and strong yet dependent upon her aid—and when she had allowed her long curls to escape he had stood silent in the presence of her womanhood. She wanted to run back and sleep in her tunnel, where the air was always moving and cool; and then in the morning, when she looked to the north, she might see the first dust of his return. She might see his tall form, and the white sides of Tellurium as he took the shortest way home, and then she could run back and drag her mother to the portal and prove that her knight had been misjudged. For her mother had predicted that the prospector would not return, and that his mine was only a blind; but she, who had seen him and felt the clasp of his hand, she knew that he would never rob *her.* So she fled to her dream-house, where there was nothing to check her fancies, and slept in the tunnel-mouth till dawn.

The day came first in the west, galloping along the Argus Range and splashing its peaks with red; and then as the sun ascended it found gaps in the eastern rim and laid long bands of light across the Sink. It rose up higher and, as the desert stood forth bare, the dweller in the dream-house stepped out through its portals and gazed long at the Death Valley Trail. From the far north pass, where it came down from Wild Rose, to where Blackwater sent up its thin smoke, the trail crept like a serpent among the sand-hills and washes, a long tenuous line through the Sink. Where the ground was white the trail stood out darker, and where it crossed the sun-burnt mesas it was white; but from one end to the other it was vacant and nothing emerged from north pass. Billy sighed and turned away, but when she came back there was a streak of dust to the south.

It came tearing along the trail from Blackwater, struck up by a galloping horseman, and at the spot where she had found the lost man the night before the flying rider stopped. He rode about in circles, started north and came dashing back; and at last, still galloping, he turned up the wash and headed for the mouth of Jail Canyon. He was some searcher who had found her tracks in the sand, and the tracks of Tellurium going on; and, rather than follow the long trail to Wild Rose Springs, he was coming to interview her. Billy ran down to meet him with long, rangey strides, and at the point of the hill she stood waiting expectantly, for visitors were rare at the ranch. Three restless lonely weeks had dragged away without bringing a single wanderer to their doors; and now here was a second man, fully as exciting as the first, because he was coming up there to see *her.* Billy tucked up her curls beneath the brim of her man's hat as she watched the laboring horse, but when she made out who it was that was coming she gave up all thought of disguise.

"Hello, Dusty!" she called running gayly down to meet him, "are you looking for Mr. Calhoun?"

"Oh, it's Mister, is it?" he yelled. "Well, have you seen the danged whelp? Whoo, boy—where is he, Billy?"

"He went back!" she cried, "I lent him my mule. He told me he'd made a rich strike!"

"A rich *strike!*" repeated the man and then he laughed and spurred his drooping mount. He was tall and bony with a thin, hawk nose and eyes sunk deep into his head. "A rich strike, eh?" he mimicked, and then he laughed again, until suddenly his face came straight. "What's that you said?" he shouted, "you didn't lend him your *mule!* Well, I'm afraid, my little girl, you've made a mistake—that feller is a regular horse-thief. Is your mother up to the house? We'll go up and see her—I'm afraid he's gone and stole your mule!"

"Oh, no he hasn't," protested Billy confidently, running along the trail beside him, "he went back to stake out his claim. He found some rich ore right there at Black Point, and he's going to give me half of it."

"At Black P'int!" whooped Dusty Rhodes doubling up in a knot to squeeze out the last atom of his mirth, "w'y I've been past that p'int for

22

twenty years—it's nothing but porphyry and burnt lava! He's crazy with the heat! Where's your father, my little girl? We'll have to go out and ketch him if we ever expect to git back that mule!"

"He's working up the canyon," answered Billy sulkily, "but never you mind about my mule. He's mine, I guess, and I loaned him to that man in exchange for a half interest in his mine!"

"Oh, it's a *mine* now, is it?" mocked Dusty Rhodes, "next thing it'll be a mine and mill. And he borrowed your mule, eh, that your father give ye, and sent ye back home on foot!"

"I don't care!" pouted Billy, "I'll bet you change your tune when you see him coming back with my mule. You went off and left him, and if I hadn't gone down and helped him he would have died in the desert of thirst."

"Eh—eh! Went off and *left* him!" bleated Dusty in a fury, "the poor fool went off and left *me!* I picked him up at Furnace Crick, over in the middle of Death Valley, and jest took him along out of pity; and all the way over he was looking at every rock when a prospector wouldn't spit on the place! He was eating my grub and packing his bed on my jacks; and then, by the gods, he wants me to stop at Black P'int while he looks at that hungry bull-quartz! I warned him distinctly that I don't wait for no man—did he say I went off and left him?"

23

"Yes, he did," answered Billy, "and he says he's going to kill you, because you went off and took all his water!"

"Hoo, hoo!" jeered Dusty Rhodes, "that big bag of wind?" But he ignored what she said about the water.

They spattered through the creek, where it flowed out to sink in the sand, and passed around the point of the canyon; and then the green valley spread out before them until it was cut off by the gorge above. This was the treacherous Corkscrew Bend, where the fury of countless cloudbursts had polished the granite walls like a tombstone; but Dusty Rhodes recalled the time when a fine stage-road had threaded its curves and led on up the canyon to old Panamint. But the flood which had destroyed the road had left the town marooned and the inhabitants had gone out over the rocks; until now only Cole Campbell, the owner of the Homestake, stayed on to do the work on his claims. In this valley far below he had made his home for years, diverting the creek to water his scanty crops; while in season and out he labored on the road which was to connect up his mine with the world.

His house stood against the hill, around the point from Corkscrew Bend, old and rambling and overgrown with vines; and along the road that led up to it there were rows of peaches and figs, fenced off by stone walls from the creek. Dusty rode past the trees slowly, feasting his eyes on their lush greenness and the rank growth of alfalfa beyond; until from the house ahead a screen door slammed and a woman gazed anxiously down.

"Oh, is that you, Mr. Rhodes?" she called out at last, "I thought it was the man who got lost! Come up to the house and tell me about him—do you think he will bring back our mule?"

He dismounted with a flourish and dropped his reins at the gate; then, while Billy hung back and petted the lathered horse, he strode up the flower-entangled walk.

"Don't think nothing, Mrs. Campbell," he announced with decision, "that boy has stole 'em before. He'll trade off that mule fer anything he can git and pull his freight fer Nevada."

He paced up to the porch and shook hands ceremoniously, after which he accepted a drink and a basketful of figs and proceeded to retail the news.

"Do you know who that feller is?" he inquired mysteriously, as Billy crept resentfully near, "he's the man that discovered the Wunpost mine and tried to keep it dark. Yes, that big mine over in Keno that they thought was worth millions, only it pinched right out at depth; but it showed up the nicest specimens of jewelry gold that has ever been seen in these parts. Well, this Wunpost, as they call him, was working on a grubstake for a banker named Judson Eells. He'd been out for two years, just sitting around the water-holes or playing coon-can with the Injuns, when he comes across this mine, or was led to it by some Injun, and he tries to cover it up. He puts up one post, to kinder hold it down in case some prospector should happen along; and then he writes his notice, *leaving out the date*—and everything else, you might say.

" 'Wunpost Mine,' " he writes, " 'John C. Calhoun owner. I claim fifteen hundred feet on this vein.'

"And jest to show you, Mrs. Campbell, what an ignorant fool he is—he spelled One Post, W-u-n! That's where he got his name!"

"I think that's a *pretty* name!" spoke up Billy loyally, as her mother joined in on the laugh. "And anyhow, just because a man can't spell, that's no reason for calling him a fool!"

"Well, he *is* a fool!" burst out Dusty Rhodes spitefully, "and more than that, he's a crook! Now that is what he done—he covered up that find and went back to the man that had grubstaked him. But this banker was no sucker, if he did have the name of staking every bum in Nevada. He was generous with his men and he give 'em all they asked for, but before he planked down a dollar he made 'em sign a contract that a corporation lawyer couldn't break. Well, when

26

Wunpost said he'd quit, Mr. Eells says all right—no hard feeling—better luck next time. But when Wunpost went back and opened up this vein Mr. Eells was Johnny-on-the-spot. He steps up to that hole and shows his contract, giving him an equal share of whatever Wunpost finds—and then he reads a clause giving him the right to take possession and to work the mine according to his judgment. And the first thing Wunpost knowed the mine was worked out and he was left holding the sack. But served him right, sez I, for trying to beat his outfitter, after eating his grub for two years!"

"But didn't he receive *anything?*" inquired Mrs. Campbell. "That seems to me pretty sharp practice."

She was a prim little woman, with honest blue eyes that sometimes made men think of their sins, and when Dusty Rhodes perceived that he had gone a bit too far he endeavored to justify his spleen.

"He received *some!*" he cried, "but what good did it do him? Eells give him five hundred dollars when he demanded an accounting and he blowed it all in in one night. He was buying the drinks for every man in camp—your money was all counterfeit with him—and the next morning he woke up without a shirt to his back, having had it torn off in a fight. What kind of a man is that to be managing a mine or to be partners with

27

a big banker like Eells? No, he walked out of camp without a cent to his name and I picked him up Tuesday over at Furnace Crick. All he had was his bed and a couple of canteens and a little jerked beef in a sack, but to hear the poor boob talk you'd think he was a millionaire—he had the world by the tail. And then, at the end of it, he'd be borrying your tobacco—or anything else you'd got. But I never would've thought that he'd steal Billy's mule—that's gitting pretty low, it strikes me."

"He never stole my mule!" burst out Wilhelmina angrily. "I expect him back here any time. And when he does come, and you hear about his mine, I'll bet you change your tune!"

"Ho! Ho!" shouted Rhodes, nodding and winking at Mrs. Campbell, "she's getting to be growed-up, ain't she? Last time I come through here she was a little girl in pigtails but now it's done up in curls. And I can't say a word against this no-account Wunpost till she calls me a liar to my face!"

"Billy is almost nineteen," answered Mrs. Campbell quietly, "but I'm surprised to hear her contradict."

"Well, I didn't mean that," apologized Wilhelmina hastily, "but—well anyhow, I *know* he's got a mine! Because he showed me a piece of quartz that he'd carried all the way, and he must have had a reason for *that*. It was just

28

moonlight, of course, and I couldn't see the gold, but I know that it was quartz."

"Ah, Billy, my little girl," returned Dusty indulgently, "you don't know the boy like I do. And the world is full of quartz but you don't find a mine right next to a well-worn trail. Have you got that piece of rock? Well now you see the p'int—he took it *away!* Would he do that if his mine was on the square?"

"Well, I don't know why not," answered Billy at last and then she bowed her head and turned away. They gazed after her pityingly as she ran along the ditch and up to the mouth of her tunnel, but Billy did not stop till she had threaded its murky passageway and come out at her gate of dreams. It was from there that she had seen him when he was lost in the Sink, and she knew her dream of dreams would come true. He was going to come back, he was going to bring her mule, and make her his partner in the mine. She looked out—and there was his dust!

CHAPTER III

DUSTY RHODES EATS DIRT

BILLY gazed away in ecstasy at the dust-cloud in the distance, and at the white spot that was Tellurium, her mule; and when the rider came closer she skipped back through the tunnel and danced along the trail to the house. Dusty Rhodes was still there, describing in windy detail Wunpost's encounter with one Pisen-face Lynch, but as she stood before them smiling he sensed the mischief in her eye and interrupted himself with a question.

"He's coming," announced Billy, showing the dimples in both cheeks and Dusty Rhodes let his jaw drop.

"Who's coming?" he asked but she dimpled enigmatically and jerked her curly head towards the road. They started up to look and as the white mule rounded the point Dusty Rhodes blinked his eyes uncertainly. After all his talk about the faithless and cowardly Wunpost here he was, coming up the road; and the memory of a canteen which he had left strapped upon a pack, rose up and left him cold. Talk as much as he would he could never escape the fact that he had gone off with Wunpost's big canteen, and the one subject he had avoided—why he had not stopped to wait for him—was now likely to be thoroughly discussed. He glanced about furtively, but there was no avenue of escape and he started off down to the gate.

"Where you been all the time?" he shouted in accusing accents, "I've been looking for you everywhere."

"Yes, you have!" thundered Wunpost dropping down off his mule and striding swiftly towards him. "You've been lapping up the booze, over at Blackwater! I've a good mind to kill you, you old dastard!"

"Didn't I tell you not to stop?" yelled Rhodes in a feigned fury. "You brought it all on yourself! I thought you'd gone back—"

"You did not!" shouted Wunpost waving his fists in the air, "you saw me behind you all the time. And if I'd ever caught up with you I'd have bashed your danged brains out, but now I'm going to let you live! I'm going to let you live so I can have a good laugh every time I see you go by—Old Dusty Rhodes, the Speed King, the Wild Ass of the Desert, the man that couldn't stop to get rich! I was running along behind you trying to make you a millionaire but you wouldn't even give me a drink! Look at *that,* what I was trying to show you!"

He whipped out a rock and slapped it into Rhodes' hand but Dusty was blind with rage.

"No good!" he said, and chucked it in the dirt

31

at which Wunpost stooped down and picked it up.

"You're a peach of a prospector," he said with biting scorn and stored it away in his pocket.

"Let me look at that again," spoke up Dusty Rhodes querulously but Wunpost had spied the ladies. He advanced to the porch, his big black hat in one hand, while he smoothed his towsled hair with the other, and the smile which he flashed Billy made her flush and then go pale, for she had neglected to change back to skirts. Every Sunday morning, and when they had visitors, she was required to don the true habiliments of her sex; but her joy at his return had left no room for thoughts of dress and she found herself in the overalls of a boy. So she stepped behind her mother and as Wunpost observed her blushes he addressed his remarks to Mrs. Campbell.

"Glad to meet you," he exclaimed with a gallantry quite surprising in a man who could not even spell "one." "I hope you'll excuse my few words with Mr. Rhodes. It's been a long time since I've had the pleasure of meeting ladies and I forgot myself for the moment. I met your daughter yesterday—good morning, Miss Wilhelmina—and I formed a high opinion of you both; because a young lady of her breeding must have a mother to be proud of, and she certainly showed she was game. She saved my life with

32

that water and lunch, and then she loaned me her mule!"

He paused and Dusty Rhodes brought his bushy eyebrows down and stabbed him to the heart with his stare.

"Lemme look at that rock!" he demanded importantly and John C. Calhoun returned his glare.

"Mr. Rhodes," he said, "after the way you have treated me I don't feel that I owe you any courtesies. You have seen the rock once and that's enough. Please excuse me, I was talking with these ladies."

"Aw, you can't fool me," burst out Dusty Rhodes vindictively, "you ain't sech a winner as you think. I've jest give Mrs. Campbell a bird's-eye view of your career, so you're coppered on that bet from the start."

"What do you mean?" demanded Wunpost drawing himself up arrogantly while his beetle-browed eyes flashed fire; but the challenge in his voice did not ring absolutely true and Dusty Rhodes grinned at him wickedly.

"You'd better learn to spell Wunpost," he said with a hectoring laugh, "before you put on any more dog with the ladies. But I asked you for that rock and I intend to git a look at it—I claim an interest in anything you've found."

"Oh, you do, eh?" returned Wunpost, now suddenly calm. "Well, let me tell you something,

Mr. Rhodes. You wasn't in my company when I found this chunk of rock, so you haven't got any interest—see? But rather than have an argument in the presence of these ladies I'll show you the quartz again."

He drew out the piece of rock and handed it to Rhodes who stared at it with sun-blinded eyes— then suddenly he whipped out a case and focused a pair of magnifying glasses meanwhile mumbling to himself in broken accents.

"Where'd you git that rock?" he asked, looking up, and Wunpost threw out his chest.

"Right there at Black Point," he answered carelessly, "you've been chasing along by it for years."

"I don't believe it!" burst out Dusty gazing wildly about and mumbling still louder in the interim. "It ain't possible—I've been right by there!"

"But perhaps you never stopped," suggested Wunpost sarcastically and handed the piece of rock to Mrs. Campbell.

"Look in them holes," he directed, "they're full of fine gold." And then he turned to Dusty.

"No, Mr. Rhodes," he said, "you ain't treated me right or I'd let you in on this strike. But you went off and left me and therefore you're out of it, and there ain't any extensions to stake. It's just a single big blow-out, an eroded volcanic cone, and I've covered it all with one claim."

"But you was *traveling* with me!" yelled Rhodes dancing about like a jay-bird, "you gimme half or I'll have the law on ye!"

"Hop to it!" invited Wunpost, "nothing would please me better than to air this whole case in court. And I'll bet, when I've finished, they'll take you out of court and hang you to the first tree they find. I'll just tell them the facts, how you went off and left me and refused to either stop or leave me water; and then I'll tell the judge how this little girl came down and saved my life with her mule. I'm not trying to play the hog—all I want is half the claim—but the other half goes to Billy. Here's the paper, Wilhelmina; I may not know how to spell but you bet your life I know who's my friend!"

He handed over a piece of the paper bag which had been used to wrap up his lunch, and as Wilhelmina looked she beheld a copy of the notice that he had posted on his claim. No knight errant of old could have excelled him in gallantry, for he had given her a full half of his claim; but her eyes filled with tears, for here, even as at Wunpost, he had betrayed his ineptitude with the pen. He had named the mine after her but he had spelled it "Willie Meena" and she knew that his detractors would laugh. Yet she folded the precious paper and thanked him shyly as he told her how to have it recorded, and then she slipped away to gloat over it alone and look through the specimen for gold.

But Dusty Rhodes, though he had been silenced for the moment, was not satisfied with the way things had gone; and while Billy was making a change to her Sunday clothes she heard his complaining voice from the corrals. He spoke as to the hilltops, after the manner of mountain men or those who address themselves to mules; and John Calhoun in turn had a truly mighty voice which wafted every word to her ears. But as she listened, half in awe at their savage repartee, a third but quieter voice broke in, and she leapt into her dress and went dashing down the hill for her father had come back from the mine. He was deaf, and slightly crippled, as the result of an explosion when his drill had struck into a missed hole; but to lonely Wilhelmina he was the dearest of companions and she shouted into his ear by the hour. And, now that he had come home, the rival claimants were laying their case before him.

Dusty Rhodes was excited, for he saw the chance of a fortune slipping away through his impotent fingers; but when Wunpost made answer he was even more excited, for the memory of his desertion rankled deep. All the ethics of the desert had been violated by Dusty Rhodes and a human life put in jeopardy, and as Wunpost dwelt upon his sufferings the old thirst for revenge rose up till it quite overmastered him. He denounced Dusty's actions in no uncertain terms, holding him up to the scorn of mankind; but Dusty was just as vehement in his impassioned defense and in his claim to a half of the strike. There the ethics of the desert came in again; for it is a tradition in mining, not unsupported by sound law, that whoever is with a man at the time of a discovery is entitled to half the find. And the hold-over from his drinking bout of the evening before made Dusty unrestrained in his protests.

The battle was at its height when Wilhelmina arrived and gave her father a hug and as the contestants beheld her, suddenly transformed to a young lady, they ceased their accusations and stood dumb. She was a child no longer, as she had appeared in the bib-overalls, but a woman and with all a woman's charm. Her eyes were very bright, her cheeks a ruddy pink, her curls a glorious halo for her head; and, standing beside her father, she took on a naive dignity that left the two fire-eaters abashed. Cole Campbell himself was a man to be reckoned with—tall and straight as an arrow, with eyes that never wavered and decision in every line of his face. His gray hair stood up straight above a brow furrowed with care and his mustache bristled out aggressively, but as he glanced down at his daughter his stern eyes suddenly softened and he acknowledged her presence with a smile.

"Are they telling you about the strike?" she called into his ear and he nodded and smiled again. "Let's go up there!" she proposed but he shook his head and turned to the expectant contestants.

"Well, gentlemen," he said, "as near as I can make out Mr. Rhodes *has* a certain right in the property. Mr. Calhoun was traveling with him and eating his grub, and I believe a court of law would decide in his favor even if he did go off and leave him in the lurch. But since my daughter picked him up and supplied him with a mule to go back and stake out the claim it might be that she also has an equity in the property, although that is for you gentlemen to decide."

"That's decided already!" shouted Wunpost angrily, "the claim has been located in her name. She's entitled to one-half and no burro-chasing prospector is going to beat her out of any part of it."

"But perhaps," suggested Campbell with a quick glance at his daughter, "perhaps she would consent to take a third. And if you would do the same that would be giving up only one sixth and yet it would obviate a lawsuit."

"Yes, and I'll sue him!" yammered Rhodes. "I'll fight him to a whisper! I'll engage the best lawyers in the country! And if I can't git it no other way—"

"That'll do!" commanded Campbell raising his

hand for peace, "there's nothing to be gained by threats. This can all be arranged if you'll just keep your heads and try to consider it impartially. I'm surprised, Mr. Rhodes, that you abandoned your pardner and left him without water on the desert. I've known you a long time and I've always respected you, but the fact would be against you in court. But on the other hand you can prove that you rode out this morning and made a diligent search, and that in itself would probably disprove abandonment, although I can't say it counts for much with me. But you've asked my opinion, gentlemen, and there it is; and my advice is to settle this matter right now without taking the case into court."

"Well, I'll give him half of my share," broke out Wunpost fretfully, "but I promised Billy half and she is going to get half—I gave her my word, and that goes."

"No, I'll give him half of mine," cried Billy to her father, "because all I did was lend him Tellurium. But before I agree to it Mr. Rhodes has got to apologize, because he said he'd steal my mule!"

"What's that?" inquired her father holding his ear down closer, "I didn't quite get that last."

"Why, Dusty Rhodes came up here to look for Mr. Calhoun, and when I told him that I had loaned him my mule he said Mr. Calhoun would *steal* him! And then he went up and told Mother all about it and said that Mr. Calhoun would do *anything,* and he said he'd probably take Tellurium to Wild Rose and trade him off to some *squaw!* And when I defended him he just whooped and laughed at me—and now he's got to *apologize!*"

She darted a hateful glance at the perspiring Dusty Rhodes, who was vainly trying to get Campbell's ear; and at the end of her recital there was a look in Wunpost's eye that spoke of reprisals to come. The fat was in the fire, as far as Rhodes was concerned, but he surprised them all by retracting. He apologized in haste, before Wunpost could make a reach for him, and then he recanted in detail, and when the tumult was over they had signed a joint agreement to give him one third of the mine.

"All right, boys," he yelled, thrusting his copy into his pocket and making a dash for his horse. "One third! It's all right with me! But if we'd gone to the courts I'd got half, sure as shooting! 'Sall right, but just watch my dust!"

CHAPTER IV

THE TREE OF LIFE

AS the evening came on they walked out together, Wunpost and the worshipful Wilhelmina, and from the portals of her House of Dreams they looked out over the Sink where they had met but the evening before. Less than a single day had passed since their stars had crossed, and already they were talking of life and eternal friendship and of all the great dreams that youth loves. Each had given of what they had without counting the cost or considering what others might say; and now they walked together like reunited lovers, though their friendship was not twenty-four hours old. Yet in that single eventful day what a gamut they had run of the emotions which make up the soul's life—of dangers boldly met, of mutual sacrifice and trust and the joys of vindication and success. They had staked all they had in the greatest game in life and, miracle of miracles, they had won. They had sought out each other's souls in the murk of death and doubt and each had been proven pure gold; yet even youth, for all its madness, has its moments of clairvoyance and Billy sensed that her joy could not last. It was too great, too perfect, to

41

endure forever, and as she gazed across the desert she sighed.

"What's the matter?" inquired Wunpost who, after a few hours' sleep, had awakened in a most expansive mood; but she only sighed again and shook her head and gazed off across the quivering Sink. It was a hell-hole of torment to those who crossed its moods and yet in that waste she had found this man, who had changed her whole outlook on life. He had come up from the desert, a sun-bronzed young giant, volcanic in his loves and his hates; and on the morrow the desert would claim him again, for he was going back to his mine. And her father was going, too—Jail Canyon would be as empty as it had been for many a long year—and she who longed to live, to plunge into the swirl of life, would be left there alone, to dream.

But what would dreams be after she had tasted the bitter-sweet of living and learned what it was that she missed; the tug of strong emotions, the hopes and fears and heartaches that are the fruits of the great Tree of Life? She wanted to pluck the fruits, be they bitter or sweet, and drain the world's wine to the dregs; and then, if life went ill, she could return to her house with something about which to dream. But now she only sighed and Wunpost took her hand and drew her down beside him in the shade.

"Don't you worry about *him* kid?" he observed

mysteriously, "I'll take care of him, all right. And don't you believe a word he said about me stealing horses and such. I'm a little rough sometimes when these jaspers try to rob me, but I never take advantage of a friend. I'm a Kentucky Calhoun, related to John Caldwell Calhoun, the great orator who debated with Webster; and a Kentucky Calhoun never forgets a kindness nor forgives an intentional injury. Dusty Rhodes thinks he's smart, getting a third of our mine after he went off and left me flat; but I'll show that old walloper before I get through with him that he can't put one over on me. And there's a man over in Nevada that's going to learn the same thing as soon as I make my stake—he's another smart Aleck that thinks he can job me and get away with highway robbery."

"Oh, is that Judson Eells?" broke in Billy quickly and Wunpost nodded his head.

"That's the hombre," he said his voice waxing louder, "he's one of these grubstake sharks. He came to Nevada after the Tonopah excitement with a flunkey they call Flip Flappum. That's another dirty dog that I'm going to put my mark on when I get him in the door—one of the most low-down, contemptible curs that I know of—he makes his living by selling bum life insurance. Phillip F. Lapham is his name but we all call him Flip Flappum—he's the black-leg lawyer that drew up that contract that made me lose my

43

mine. Did Dusty tell you about it—then he told you a lie—I never even read the cussed contract! I was broke, to tell you the truth, and I'd have signed my own death warrant to get the price of a plate of beans; and so I put my name in the place where he told me and never thought nothing about it.

"It was a grubstake, that's all I knew, giving him half of what I staked in exchange for what I could eat; but it turned out afterwards it was like these fire insurance policies, where a man never reads the fine print. There was more jokers in that contract than in a tinhorn gambler's deck of cards—he had me peoned for life—and after I'd given him half my strike he came out and claimed it all. Well, no man would stand for that but when I went to make a kick there was a rat-faced guard there waiting for me. Pisen-face Lynch they call him, and if he was half as bad as he looks he'd be the wild wolf of the world; but he ain't, not by a long shot, he just had the drop on me, and he run me off my own claim! I came back and they ganged me and when I woke up I looked like I'd been through a barbed-wire fence.

"Well, after that, as the nigger says, I began to think they didn't want me around there, and so I pulled my freight; and it wasn't a month afterwards that the ore all pinched out and left Judson Eells belly up. If he lost one dollar I'll bet he lost fifty thousand, besides tipping his hand on that contract; and I walked clean back from the lower end of Death Valley just to see how his lip was hung. He's a big, fat slob, and when times are good he goes around with his lip pulled up, so! But this time he looked like an old muley cow that's come through a long, late spring—his lip was plumb down on his brisket. So I gave him the horse-laugh, paid my regards to Flip and Lynch, and came away feeling fine. Because I'll tell you Billy, sure as God made little fishes, there's a hereafter coming to them three men; and I'm the boy that's going to deal 'em the misery—you wait, and watch my smoke!"

He smiled benevolently into Billy's startled eyes, and as the subject seemed to interest her he settled himself more comfortably and proceeded with his views on life.

"Yes sir," he said, "I'll put a torch under them, that'll burn 'em off the face of the earth. Did you ever see a banker that wasn't a regular robber— with special attention to widows and orphans? Well, take it from me, Billy, they're a bunch of crooks—I guess I ought to know. I was just eleven years old when they foreclosed the mortgage and turned my mother and us kids into the street; and since then I've done everything from punching cows to highway robbery but I've never forgot those bankers. That's how come I signed up with Judson Eells, I thought I was

45

sticking him good; but he was playing a system and they didn't anybody tumble to it until I discovered the Wunpost.

"W'y, there wasn't a prospector in the state of Nevada that hadn't worked old Eells for a grubstake. We thought he was easy, kind of bugs on mining like all the rest of these nuts, but the minute I struck the Wunpost—*bing,* he's there with his contract and we find where we've all been stung. We're tied up, by grab, with more whereases and wherefores, and the parties of the first part, and so on, than you'd find in a book of law; and the boys all found out from what he did to me that he had us euchered at every turn. I thought I could fool him by covering up the hole—"

"Oh, did you do that!" burst out Billy reproachfully, "and I made Dusty Rhodes apologize!"

"Never mind," said Wunpost, "that was nothing but jaw-bone. He just said it to get a share in our mine."

"No, but listen," protested Billy, "that isn't what I mean. Do you think it was right to deceive Eells?"

"Was it *right,* kid!" laughed Wunpost. "That ain't nothing to what I'm *going* to do if I ever get the chance. Didn't he hire that black-leg lawyer to draw up a cinch contract with the purpose of grabbing all I found? Well then, that shows how

46

honest *he* was—and now I'm out after his scalp. I've got to raise a stake, so I can fight him dollar for dollar; and then, sure as shooting, I'm going to bust his bank and make him walk out of camp. Was it right—say, that's a good one—you ain't been around much, have you? Well, that's all right, Billy; I like you, all the same."

He nodded approvingly and Billy sat staring, for her world had gone topsy-turvy again. She had wanted to leave Jail Canyon and go out into the world, but was it possible that there existed a state of society where there was no right and wrong? She sat thinking a minute, her head in a whirl, and then she came back again.

"But when you covered up this mine and tried to keep it for yourself, he—had Mr. Eells ever done you any harm?"

"Well, not yet, kid—that is, I didn't know it— but believe me, his intentions were good. The time hadn't come, that's all."

"He was your friend, then," contended Billy, "because Dusty Rhodes said—"

"Dusty Rhodes!" bellowed Wunpost and then he paused. "Go on, let's get this off your chest."

"Well, he said," continued Billy, "that Mr. Eells gave you everything and that you lived off his grubstake for two years; so I don't think it was right, when you finally found a mine—"

"Say, listen," broke in Wunpost leaning over and tapping her on the knee while he fixed her with intolerant eyes, "who's your friend, now—Dusty Rhodes or me?"

"Why—you are," faltered Billy, "but I don't see—"

"All right then," pronounced Wunpost, "if I'm your friend, *stay with me*. Don't tell me what Dusty Rhodes said!"

"That's all right," she defended, "didn't I make him apologize? But I'm *your* friend, too, and I don't think it was right—"

"Right!" thundered Wunpost, "where do you get this 'right' stuff? Have you lived up this canyon all your life? Well, you wait until tomorrow, when the rush is on, and I'll show you how much *right* there is in mining! You come down to the mine and I'll show you a bunch of mugs that would rob you of your claim like *that!* I'm going to be there, myself, and I'm going to borrow that pistol that you stuck in my ribs the other night; and the first yap that touches a corner or crosses my line I'll make him hard to catch. And then will come the promoters, with their diamonds and certified checks, and they'll offer you millions and millions; but you stay with me, kid, if they offer you the sub-treasury, because they'll clean you if you ever sign up. Don't sign nothing, see—and don't promise anything, either; and I'll tell you about *me,* I'll do anything for a friend—but that's as far as I go. They ain't no right and wrong, as far as I'm

48

concerned. I'm like a danged Injun, I'll keep my word to a friend no matter how the cards fall; but if that friend turns against me I'll scalp him like *that,* and hang his hide on the fence! So now you know right where you'll find me!"

"Well, all right," retorted Billy, whose Scotch blood was up, "and I'll tell you right where you'll find *me.* I'll stay with my friends whether they're right or wrong, but I'll never do anything dishonest. And if you don't like that you can take back your claim because—"

"Sure I like it!" cried Wunpost, laughing and patting her hand, "that's just the kind of a friend I want. But all the same, Billy, this is no Sunday school picnic—it's more like a dog fight we're going to—and the only way to stand off that bunch of burglars is to hit 'em with anything you've got. You've got to grab with both hands and kick with both feet if you want to win in this mining game; and when you try to fight honest you're tying one hand behind you, because some of 'em won't stop at murder. Eells and Flip Flap and their kind don't pretend to be honest, they just get by with the law; and if you give 'em the edge they'll soak you in the jaw the first time you turn your head."

"Well, I don't care," returned Billy, "my father is honest and nobody ever robbed him of his claim!"

"Hooh! Who wants it?" jeered Wunpost

arrogantly. "I'm talking about a real mine. Your old man's claims are stuck up in a canyon where a flying machine couldn't hardly go and about the time he gets his road built another cloudburst will come along and wash it away. Oh, don't talk to me, I *know*—I've been all along those peaks and right down past his mine—and I tell you it isn't worth stealing!"

"And I've been up there, too, and helped pack out the ore, and I tell you you don't know what you're talking about!"

Billy's eyes flashed dangerously as she sprang up to face him and for a minute they matched their wills; then Wunpost laughed shortly and stepped out into the open where the sun was just topping the mountains.

"Well all right, kid," he said, "have your own way about it. It makes no difference to me."

"No, I guess not," retorted Billy, "or you'd find out what you were talking about before you said that my father was a fool. His mine is just as good as it ever was—all it needs is another road."

"Yes, and then *another* road," chimed in Wunpost mockingly, "as soon as the first cloudburst comes by. And the price of silver is just half what it was when Old Panamint was on the boom. But that makes no difference, of course?"

"Yes, it does," acknowledged Billy whose eyes

were gray with rage, "but the flotation process is so much cheaper than milling that it more than evens things up. And there hasn't been a cloudburst in thirteen years—but that makes no difference, of course!"

She spat it out spitefully and Wunpost curbed his wit for he saw where his jesting was leading to. When it came to her father this unsophisticated child would stand up and fight like a wildcat. And he began to perceive too that she was not such a child—she was a woman, with the experience of a child. In the ways of the world she was a mere babe in the woods but in intellect and character she was far from being dwarfed and her honesty was positively embarrassing. It crowded him into corners that were hard to get out of and forced him to make excuses for himself, whereas at the moment he was all lit up with joy over the miracle of his second big strike. He had discovered the Wunpost, and lost it on a fluke; but the Willie Meena was different—if he kept the peace with her they would both come out with a fortune.

"Never mind now, kid," he said at last, "your father is all right—I like him. And if he thinks he can get rich by building roads up the canyon, that's his privilege; it's nothing to me. But you string along with me on our mine down below and there'll be money and to spare for us both; and then you can take your share and build the

51

old man a road that'll make 'em all take notice! About twenty thousand dollars ought to fix the matter up, but if we get to gee-hawing and Dusty Rhodes mixes in there won't be a dollar for any of us. We've got to stand together, see—you and me against old Dusty—and that will give us control."

"Well, I didn't start the quarrel," said Billy, beginning to blink, "but it makes me mad, just because father won't give up to have everybody saying he's crazy. But he isn't—he knows just exactly what he's doing—and some day he'll be a rich man when these Blackwater pocket-miners are destitute. The Homestake mine produced half a million dollars, the second time they opened it up, and if the road hadn't washed out it would be producing yet and my father would be rated a millionaire. If he would sell out his claims, or just organize a company and give outside capitalists control—"

"Don't you do it!" warned Wunpost, who made a very poor listener, "they'll skin you, every time. The party that has control can take over the property and exclude the minority stockholders from the ground, and all they can do is to sue for an accounting and demand a look at the books. But the books are nothing, it's what's underground that counts, and if you try to go down they can kill you. I learned that from Judson Eells when he put me out of Wunpost—and say, we can work that on Dusty! We'll treat him white at first, but the minute he gets gay, it's the gate—we'll give him the gate!"

He pranced about joyously, vainly trying to make her smile, but Wilhelmina had lost her gaiety.

"No," she said, "let's not do that—because I made him apologize, you know. But don't you think it's possible that Judson Eells will follow after you and claim this mine too, under his contract?"

"He can't!" chuckled Wunpost starting to do a double-shuffle, "I fooled him—this isn't Nevada. And when I found the Wunpost I was eating his grub, but this time I was strictly on my own. I came to a country where I'd never been before, so he couldn't say I'd covered it up; and that contract was made out in the state of Nevada, but this is clear over in California. Not a chance, kid, we're rich, cheer up!"

He tried to grab her hand but she drew it away from him and an anxious look crept into her eyes.

"No," she said, "let's not be foolish." Already the great dream had sped.

53

CHAPTER V

THE WILLIE MEENA

THE morning had scarcely dawned when Wilhelmina dashed up the trail and looked down on the Sink below; and Wunpost had been right, where before all was empty, now the Death Valley Trail was alive. From Blackwater to Wild Rose Wash the dust rose up in clouds, each streamer boring on towards the north; and already the first stampeders had passed out of sight in their rush for the Black Point strike. It lay beyond North Pass, cut off from view by the shoulder of a long, low ridge; but there it was, and her claim and Wunpost's was already swarming with men. The whole town of Blackwater had risen up in the night and gone streaking across the Sink, and what was to keep those envious pocket-miners from claiming the find for their own? And Dusty Rhodes—he must have led the stampede—had he respected his partners' rights? She gazed a long moment, then darted back through the tunnel and bore the news to her father and Wunpost.

He had slept in the hay, this hardy desert animal, this shabby, penniless man with the loud voice of a demagogue and the profile of a bronze Greek god; and he came forth boldly, like

Odysseus of old when, cast ashore on a strange land, he roused from his sleep and beheld Nausicaa and her maidens at play. But as Nausicaa, the princess, withstood his advance when all her maidens had fled, so Wilhelmina faced him, for she knew full well now that he was not a god. He was a water-hole prospector who for two idle years had eaten the bread of Judson Eells; and then, when chance led him to a rich vein of ore, had covered up the hole and said nothing. Yet for all his human weaknesses he had one godlike quality, a regal disregard for wealth; for he had kept his plighted word and divided, half and half, this mine towards which all Blackwater now rushed. She looked at him again and her rosy lips parted—he had earned the meed of a smile.

The day had dawned auspiciously, as far as Billy was concerned, for she was back in her overalls and her father had consented to take her along to the mine. The claim was part hers and Wunpost had insisted that she accompany them back to the strike. Dusty Rhodes would be there, with his noisy demands and his hints at greater rights in the claim; and in the first wild rush complications might arise that would call for a speedy settlement. But with Billy at his side and Cole Campbell as a witness, every detail of their agreement could be proved on the instant and the Willie Meena started off right. So Wunpost smiled back when he beheld the make-believe boy who had come to his aid on her mule; and as they rode off down the canyon, driving four burros, two packed with water, he looked her over approvingly.

In skirts she had something of the conventional reserve which had always made him scared of women; but as a boy, as Billy, she was one partner in a thousand, and as carefree as the wind. Upon the back of her saddle, neatly tied up in a bag, she carried the dress that she would wear at the mine; but riding across the mesa on the lonely Indian trail she clung to the garb of utility. In overalls she had ridden up and down the corkscrew canyon that led to her father's mine; she had gone out to hunt for burros, dragged in wood and carried up water and done the daily duties of a man. Both her brothers were gone, off working in the mines, and their tasks descended to her; until in stride and manner and speech she was by instinct, a man and only by thought a woman.

The years had slipped by, even her mother had hardly noticed how she too had grown up like the rest; and now in one day she had stepped forth into their councils and claimed her place as a man. Yes, that was the place that she had instinctively claimed but they had given her the place of a woman. When it came to prospecting among the lonely peaks she could go as far as she

56

chose; but in the presence of men, even as an owner in the great mine, she must confine her free limbs within skirts. And, though she had come of age, she was still in tutelage—with two men along to do her thinking. Wunpost had made it easy, all she had to do was stand pat and agree to whatever he said; and her father was there to protect her in her rights and preserve the family honor from loose tongues.

They skirted the edge of the valley, keeping up above the Sink and crossing an endless series of rocky washes, until as they topped the last low ridge the Black Point lay before them, surrounded by a swarm of digging men. It jutted out from the ridge, a round volcanic cone sticking up through the shattered porphyry; and yet this point of rock, all but buried in the wash of centuries, held a treasure fit to ransom a king. It held the Willie Meena mine, which had lain there by the trail while thousands of adventurers hurried past; until at last Wunpost had stopped to examine it and had all but perished of thirst. But one there was who had seen him, and saved him from the Sink, and loaned him her mule to ride; and in honor of her, though he could not spell her name, he had called it the Willie Meena.

Billy sat on Tellurium and gazed with rapt wonder at the scene which stretched out below. Wagons and horses everywhere, and automobiles too, and dejected-looking burros and mules; and in the rough hills beyond men were climbing like goats as they staked the lava-crowned buttes. A procession of Indian wagons was filing up the gulch to haul water from Wild Rose Spring and already the first tent of what would soon be a city was set up opposite the point. In a few hours there would be twenty up, in a few days a hundred, in a few months it would be a town; and all named for her, who had been given a half by Wunpost and yet had hardly murmured her thanks. She turned to him smiling but as she was about to speak her father caught her eye.

"Put on your dress," he said, and she retired, red with chagrin, to struggle into that accursed badge of servitude. It was hot, the sun boiled down as it does every day in that land where the rocks are burned black; and, once she was dressed, she could not mount her mule without seeming to be immodest. So she followed along behind them, leading Tellurium by his rope, and entered her city of dreams unnoticed. Calhoun strode on before her, while Campbell rounded up the burros, and the men from Blackwater stared at him. He was a stranger to them all, but evidently not to boom camps, for he headed for the solitary tent.

"Good morning to you, gentlemen," he called out in his great voice; "won't you join me—let's all have a drink!"

The crowd fell in behind him, another crowd

58

opened up in front, and he stood against the bar, a board strewn thick with glasses and tottering bottles of whiskey. An old man stood behind it, wagging his beard as he chewed tobacco, and as he set out the glasses he glanced up at Wunpost with a curious, embittered smile. He was white-faced and white-bearded, stooped and gnarled like a wind-tortured tree, and the crook to his nose made one think instinctively of pictures of the Wandering Jew. Or perhaps it was the black skull-cap, set far back on his bent head, which gave him the Jewish cast; but his manner was that of the rough-and-ready barkeeper and he slapped one wet hand on the bar.

"Here's to her!" cried Wunpost, ignoring the hint to pay as he raised his glass to the crowd. "Here's to the Willie Meena—some mine!"

He tossed off the drink, but when he looked for the chaser the barkeeper shook his head.

"No chasers," he said, "water is too blasted scarce—that'll be three dollars and twenty-five cents."

"Charge it to ground-rent!" grinned Wunpost. "I'm the man that owns this claim. See you later—where's Dusty Rhodes?"

"No—*cash!*" demanded the barkeeper, looking him coldly in the eye. "I'm in on this claim myself."

"Since when?" inquired Wunpost. "Maybe you don't know who I am? I am John C. Calhoun, the

59

man that discovered Wunpost; and unless I'm greatly mistaken you're not in on anything—who gave you any title to this ground?"

"Dusty Rhodes," croaked the saloon-keeper, and a curse slipped past Wunpost's lips, though he knew that a lady was near.

"Well, damn Dusty Rhodes!" he cried in a passion. "Where is the crazy fool?"

He burst from the crowd just as Dusty came hurrying across from where he had been digging out ore; and for a minute they stood clamoring, both shouting at once, until at last Wunpost seized him by the throat.

"Who's this old stiff with whiskers?" he yelled into his ear, "that thinks he owns the whole claim? Speak up, or I'll wring your neck!"

He released his hold and Dusty Rhodes staggered back, while the crowd looked on in alarm.

"W'y, that's Whiskers," explained Dusty, "the saloon-keeper down in Blackwater. I guess I didn't tell you but he give me a grubstake and so he gits half my claim."

"*Your* claim!" echoed Wunpost. "Since when was this your claim? You doddering old tarrapin, you only own one-third of it—and that ain't yours, by rights. How much do you claim, I say?"

"W'y—I only claim one-third," responded Dusty weakly, "but Whiskers, he claims that I'm entitled to a half—"

"A half!" raged Wunpost, starting back towards the saloon. "I'll show the old billygoat what he owns!"

He kicked over the bar with savage destructiveness, jerking up a tent-peg with each brawny hand, and as the old man cowered he dragged the tent forward until it threatened every moment to come down.

"Git out of here!" he ordered, "git off of my ground! I discovered this claim and it's located in my name—now git, before I break you in two!"

"Here, here!" broke in Cole Campbell, laying a hand on Wunpost's arm as the saloon-keeper began suddenly to beg, "let's not have any violence. What's the trouble?"

"Why, this old spittoon-trammer," began Wunpost in a fury, "has got the nerve to claim half my ground. I've been beat out of one claim, but this time it's different—I'll show him who owns this ground!"

"I just claim a quarter of it!" snapped old Whiskers vindictively. "I claim half of Dusty Rhodes' share. He was working on my grubstake—and he was with you when you made your strike."

"He was not!" denied Wunpost, "he went off and left me. Did you find his name on the notice? No, you found John C. Calhoun and Williemeena Campbell, the girl that loaned me her mule.

61

We're the locators of this property, and, just to keep the peace, we agreed to give Dusty one third; but that ain't a half and if you say it is again, out you go—I'll throw you off my claim!"

"Well, a third, then," screeched Old Whiskers, holding his hands about his ears, "but for cripes' sake quit jerking that tent! Ain't a third enough to give me a right to put up my tent on the ground?"

"It is if I say so," replied Wunpost authoritatively, "and if Williemeena Campbell consents. But git it straight now—we're running this property and you and Dusty are *nothing*. You're the minority, see, and if you make a crooked move we'll put you both off the claim. Can you git that through your head?"

"Well, I guess so," grumbled Whiskers, stooping to straighten up his bar, and Wunpost winked at the crowd.

"Set 'em up again!" he commanded regally and all Blackwater drank on the house.

CHAPTER VI

CINCHED

HAVING established his rights beyond the peradventure of a doubt, the imperious Wunpost left Old Whiskers to recoup his losses and turned to the wide-eyed Wilhelmina. She had been standing, rooted to the earth, while he assaulted Old Whiskers and Rhodes; and as she glanced up at him doubtfully he winked and grinned back at her and spoke from behind the cover of his hand.

"That's the system!" he said. "Git the jump on 'em—treat 'em rough! Come on, let's go look at our mine!"

He led the way to Black Point, where the bonanza vein of quartz came down and was buried in the sand; and while the crowd gazed from afar they looked over their property, though Billy moved like one in a dream. Her father was engaged in placating Dusty Rhodes and in explaining their agreement to the rest, and she still felt surprised that she had ever consented to accompany so desperate a ruffian. Yet as he knocked off a chunk of ore and showed her the specks of gold, scattered through it with such prodigal richness, she felt her old sense of security return; for he had never been rough with

63

her. It was only with Old Whiskers, the grasping Blackwater saloon-keeper, and with the equally avaricious Dusty Rhodes—who had been trying to steal more than their share of the prospect and to beat her out of her third. They had thought to ignore her, to brush her aside and usurp her share in the claim; but Wunpost had defended her and protected her rights and put them back where they belonged. And it was for this that he had seized Dusty Rhodes by the throat and kicked down the saloon-keeper's bar. But she wondered what would happen if, at some future time, she should venture to oppose his will.

The vein of quartz which had caught Wunpost's eye was enclosed within another, not so rich, and a third mighty ledge of low-grade ore encased the two of them within its walls. This big dyke it was which formed the backbone of the point, thrusting up through the half-eroded porphyry; and as it ran up towards its apex it was swallowed and overcapped by the lava from the old volcanic cone.

"Look at that!" exclaimed Wunpost, knocking off chunk after chunk; and as a crowd began to gather he dug down on the richest streak, giving the specimens to the first person who asked. The heat beat down upon them and Campbell called Wilhelmina to the shelter of his makeshift tent, but on the ledge Wunpost dug on untiringly while the pocket-miners gathered about. They

64

knew, if he did not, the value of those rocks which he dispensed like so much dirt, and when he was not looking they gathered up the leavings and even knocked off more for themselves. There had been hungry times in the Blackwater district, and some of this quartz was half gold.

An Indian wood-hauler came down from Wild Rose Spring with his wagon filled with casks of water, and as he peddled his load at two-bits a bucket the camp took on a new lease of life. Old Whiskers served a chaser with each drink of whiskey; coffee was boiled and cooking began; and all the drooping horses were banded together and driven up the canyon to the spring. It was only nine miles, and the Indians would keep on hauling, but already Wunpost had planned to put in a pipe-line and make Willie Meena a town. He stood by Campbell's tent while the crowd gathered about and related the history of his strike, and then he went on with his plans for the mine and his predictions of boom times to come.

"Just you wait," he said, bulking big in the moonlight; "you wait till them Nevada boomers come. Things are dead over there—Keno and Wunpost are worked out; they'll hit for this camp to a man. And when they come, gentlemen, you want to be on your ground, because they'll jump anything that ain't held down. Just wait till they see this ore and then watch their dust—they'll stake the whole country for miles—but I've only got one claim, and I'm going to stay on it, and the first man that jumps it will get this."

He slapped the big pistol that he had borrowed from Wilhelmina and nodded impressively to the crowd; and the next morning early he was over at the hole, getting ready for the rush that was to come. For the news of the strike had gone out from Blackwater on the stage of the evening before, and the moment it reached the railroad it would be wired to Keno and to Tonopah and Goldfield beyond. Then the stampede would begin, over the hills and down into Death Valley and up Emigrant Wash to the springs; and from there the first automobiles would burn up the ground till they struck Wild Rose Canyon and came down. Wunpost got out a hammer and drill, and as he watched for the rush he dug out more specimens to show. Wilhelmina stood beside him, putting the best of them into an ore-sack and piling the rest on the dump; and as he met her glad smile he laid down his tools and nodded at her wisely.

"Big doings, kid," he said. "There's some rock that'll make 'em scream. D'ye remember what I said about Dusty Rhodes? Well, maybe I didn't call the turn—he did just exactly what I said. When he got to Blackwater he claimed the strike was his and framed it up with Whiskers to freeze us out. They thought they had us jumped—somebody knocked down my

66

monument, and that's a State Prison offense—but I came back at 'em so quick they were whipped before they knew it. They acknowledged that the claim was mine. Well, all right, kid, let's keep it; you tag right along with me and back up any play that I make, and if any of these boomers from Nevada get funny we'll give 'em the gate, the gate!"

He did a little dance and Billy smiled back feebly, for it was all very bewildering to her. She had expected, of course, a certain amount of lawless conduct; but that Dusty Rhodes, an old friend of their family, should conspire to deprive her of her claim was almost inconceivable. And that Wunpost should instantly seize him by the throat and force him to renounce his claims was even more surprising. But of course he had warned her, he had told her all about it, and predicted even bolder attempts; and yet here he was, digging out the best of his ore to give to these same Nevada burglars.

"What do you give them all the ore for?" she asked at last. "Why don't you keep it, and we can pound out the gold?"

"We have to play the game, kid," he answered with a shrug. "That's the way they always do."

"Yes, but I should think it would only make them worse. When they see how rich it is maybe someone will try to jump us—do you think Judson Eells will come?"

67

"Sure he'll come," answered Wunpost. "He'll be one of the first."

"And will you give him a specimen?"

"Surest thing—I'll give him a good one. I believe that's a machine, up the wash."

He shaded his eyes, and as they gazed up the winding canyon a monster automobile swung around the curve. A flash and it was gone, only to rush into view a second time and come bubbling and thundering down the wash. It drew up before the point and four men leapt out and headed straight for the hole; not a word was said, but they seemed to know by instinct just where to find the mine. Wunpost strode to meet them and greeted them by name, they came up and looked at the ground; and then, as another machine came around the point, they asked him his price, for cash.

"Nothing doing, gentlemen," answered Wunpost. "It's too good to sell. It'll pay from the first day it's worked."

He went down to meet the second car of stampeders, and his answer to them was the same. And each time he said it he turned to Wilhelmina, who gravely nodded her head. It was his mine; he had found it and only given her a share of it, and of course they must stand together; but as machine after machine came whirling down the canyon and the bids mounted higher and higher a wistful look came into

Wilhelmina's eye and she went down and sat with her father. It was for him that she wanted the money that was offered her—to help him finish the road he had been working on so long—but she did not speak, and he too sat silent, looking on with brooding eyes. Something seemed to tell them both that trouble was at hand, and when, after the first rush, a single auto rumbled in, Billy rose to her feet apprehensively. A big man with red cheeks, attired in a long linen duster, descended from the curtained machine, and she flew to the side of Wunpost.

It was Judson Eells; she would know him anywhere from the description that Wunpost had given, and as he came towards the hole she took in every detail of this man who was predestined to be her enemy. He was big and fat, with a high George the Third nose and the florid smugness of a country squire, and as he returned Wunpost's greeting his pendulous lower lip was thrust up in arrogant scorn. He came on confidently, and behind him like a shadow there followed a mysterious second person. His nose was high and thin, his cheeks gaunt and furrowed, and his eyes seemed brooding over some terrible wrong which had turned him against all mankind. At first glance his face was terrifying in its fierceness, and then the very badness of it gave the effect of a caricature. His eyebrows were too black, his lips too grim, his jaw too firmly set;

and his haggard eyes looked like those of a woman who is about to burst into hysterical tears. It was Pisen-face Lynch, and as Wunpost caught his eye he gave way to a mocking smirk.

"Ah, good morning, Mr. Eells," he called out cordially, "good morning, good morning Mr. Lynch! Well, well, glad to see you—how's the bad man from Bodie? Meet my partner, Miss Wilhelmina Campbell!"

He presented her gallantly and as Wilhelmina bowed she felt their hostile eyes upon her.

"Like to look at our mine?" rattled on Wunpost affably. "Well, here it is, and she's a world-beater. Take a squint at that rock—you won't need no glasses—how's that, Mr. Eells, for the pure quill?"

Eells looked at the specimen, then looked at it again, and slipped it into his pocket.

"Yes, rich," he said in a deep bass voice, "very rich—it looks like a mine. But—er—did I understand you to say that Miss Campbell was your partner? Because really you know—"

"Yes, she's my partner," replied Wunpost. "We hold the controlling interest. Got a couple more partners that own a third."

"Because really," protested Eells, "under the terms of our contract—"

"Oh, to hell with your contract!" burst out Wunpost scornfully. "Do you think that will hold over here?"

70

"Why, undoubtedly!" exclaimed Eells. "I hope you didn't think—but no matter, I claim half of this mine."

"You won't get it," answered Wunpost. "This is over in California. Your contract was made for Nevada."

"It was made *in* Nevada," corrected Judson Eells promptly, "but it applied to all claims, *wherever found!* Would you like to see a copy of the contract?" He turned to the automobile, and like a jack-in-the-box a little lean man popped out.

"No!" roared Wunpost, and looked about wildly, at which Cole Campbell stepped up beside him.

"What's the trouble?" he asked, and as Wunpost shouted into his ear Campbell shook his head and smiled dubiously.

"Let's look at the contract," he suggested, and Wunpost, all unstrung, consented. Then he grabbed him back and yelled into his ear:

"*That's* no good now—he's used it once already!"

"How do you mean?" queried Campbell, still reaching for the contract; and the jack-in-the-box thrust it into his hands.

"Why, he used that same paper to claim the Wunpost—he can't claim every mine I find!"

"Well, we'll see," returned Campbell, putting on his glasses, and Wunpost flew into a fury.

71

"Git out of here!" he yelled, making a kick at Pisen-face Lynch; "git out, or I'll be the death of ye!"

But Pisen-face Lynch recoiled like a rattle-snake and stood set with a gun in each hand.

"Don't you think it," he rasped, and Wunpost turned away from him with a groan of mortal agony.

"What does it say?" he demanded of Campbell. "Can he claim this mine, too? But say, listen; I wasn't *working* for him! I was working for myself, and furnishing my own grub—and I've never been through here before! He can't claim I found it when I was under his grubstake, because I've never been into this country!"

He stopped, all a-tremble, and looked on helplessly while Cole Campbell read on through the "fine print"; and, not being able to read the words, he watched the face of the deaf man like a criminal who hopes for a reprieve. But there was no reprieve for Wunpost, for the paper he had signed made provision against every possible contingency; and the man who had drawn it stood there smiling triumphantly—the jack-in-the-box was none other than Lapham. Wunpost watched till he saw his last hope flicker out, then whirled on the gloating lawyer. Phillip F. Lapham was tall and thin, with the bloodless pallor of a lunger, but as Wunpost began to curse him a red spot mounted to each cheek-bone and he pointed his lanky forefinger like a weapon.

"Don't you threaten me!" he cried out vindictively, "or I'll have you put under bond. The fault is your own if you failed to read this contract, or failed to understand its intent. But there it stands, a paper of record and unbeatable in any court in the land. I challenge you to break it—every provision is reciprocal—it is sound both in law and equity! And under clause seven my client, Mr. Eells, is entitled to one-half of this claim!"

"But I only own one-third of it!" protested Wunpost desperately. "I located it for myself and Wilhelmina Campbell, and then we gave Dusty Rhodes a third."

"That's beside the point," answered Lapham briefly. "If you were the original and sole discoverer, Mr. Eells is entitled to one-half, and any agreements which you have made with others will have to be modified accordingly."

"What do you mean?" yelled a voice, and Dusty Rhodes, who had been listening, now jumped into the center of the arena. "I'll have you to understand," he cried in a fury, "that I'm entitled to a full half in this claim. I was with this man Wunpost when he made the discovery, and according to mining law I'm entitled to one-half of it—I don't give *that* for you and your contract!"

73

He snapped his fingers under the lawyer's nose and Lapham drew back, startled.

"Then in that case," stated Wunpost, "I don't get *anything*—and I'm the man that discovered it! But I'll tell you, my merry men, there's another law yet, when a man is sure he's right!"

He tapped his six-shooter and even Lynch blenched, for the fighting light had come into his eyes. "No," went on Wunpost, "you can't work that on me. I found this mine and I'm going to have half of it or shoot it out with the bunch of ye!"

"You can have my share," interposed Wilhelmina tremulously, and he flinched as if struck by a whip.

"I don't want it!" he snarled. "It's these high-binders I'm after. You, Dusty, you don't get anything now. If this big fat slob is going to claim half my mine, you can *law* us—he'll have to pay the bills. Now git, you old dastard, and if you horn in here again I'll show you where you head *out!*" He waved him away, and Dusty Rhodes slunk off, for a guilty conscience makes cowards of us all; but Judson Eells stood solid as adamant, though his lawyer was whispering in his ear.

"Go and see him," nodded Eells, and as Lapham followed Rhodes he turned to the excited Wunpost.

"Mr. Calhoun," he began, "I see no reason to

withdraw from my position in regard to this claim. This contract is legal and was made in good faith, and moreover I can prove that I paid out two thousand dollars before you ever located a claim. But all that can be settled in court. If you have given Miss Campbell a third, her share is now a sixth, because only half of the mine was yours to give; and so on with the rest, though if Mr. Rhodes' claim is valid we will allow him his original one-third. Now what would you say if I should allow *you* one-third, of which you can give Miss Campbell what you wish, and I will keep the other, allowing Mr. Rhodes the last— each one of us to hold a third interest?"

"I would say—" burst out Wunpost, and then he stopped, for Wilhelmina was tugging at his arm. She spoke quickly into his ear, he flared up and then subsided, and at last he turned sulkily to Eells.

"All right," he said, "I'll take the third. I see you've got me cinched."

CHAPTER VII

MORE DREAMS

In four days' time Wunpost had seen his interest dwindle from full ownership to a mere sixth of the Willie Meena. First he had given Billy half, then they had each given Rhodes a sixth; and now Judson Eells had stepped in with his contract and trimmed their holdings by a half. In another day or so, if the ratio kept up, Wunpost's sixth would be reduced to a twelfth, a twenty-fourth, a forty-eighth, a ninety-sixth—and he had discovered the mine himself! What philosophy or sophistry can reconcile a man to such buffets from the hand of Fate? Wunpost cursed and turned to raw whiskey. It was the infamy of it all; the humiliation, the disgrace, the insult of being trimmed by a lawyer—twice! Yes, twice in the same place, with the same contract, the same system; and now this same Flip Flappum was busy as a hunting dog trying to hire one of his partners to sell him out!

Wunpost towered above Old Whiskers, and so terrible was his presence that the saloon-keeper never hinted at pay. He poured out drink after drink of the vitriolic whiskey, which Whiskers made in the secrecy of his back-room; and as Wunpost drank and shuddered the waspish

Phillip F. Lapham set about his complete undoing. First he went to Dusty Rhodes, who still claimed a full half, and browbeat him until he fell back to a third; and then, when Dusty priced his third at one million, he turned to the disillusioned Billy. Her ideas were more moderate, as far as values were concerned, but her loyalty to Wunpost was still unshaken and she refused to even consider a sale. Back and forth went the lawyer like a shuttle in its socket, from Dusty Rhodes to Wilhelmina and then back once more to Rhodes; but Dusty would sign nothing, sell nothing, agree to nothing, and Billy was almost as bad. She placed a cash value of twenty thousand dollars on her interest in the Willie Meena Mine, but the sale was contingent upon the consent of John C. Calhoun, who had drowned his sorrows at last. So they waited until morning and Billy laid the matter before him when her father brought the drunken man to their tent.

Wunpost was more than drunk, he was drugged and robbed of reason by the poison which Old Whiskers had brewed; but even with this handicap his mind leapt straight to the point and he replied with an emphatic "No!"

"Twenty thousand!" he repeated, "twenty thousand devils—twenty thousand little demons from hell! What do you want to sell me out for—didn't I give you your interest? Well, listen, kid—you ever been to school? Then how much is one-sixth and one-third—add 'em together! Makes *three*-sixths, don't it—well, ain't that a half? I ain't educated, that's all right; but I can *think,* kid, can't I? Flip Flappum he wants to get control. Give him a half, under my contract, and he can take possession—and then where do *I* git off? I git off at the same place I got off over at Wunpost; he's trying to freeze me out. So if you want to do me dirt, kid, when I've always been your friend, go to it and sell him your share. Take your paltry twenty thousand and let old Wunpost rustle—serves him right, the poor, ignorant fool!"

He swayed about and Billy drew away from him, but her answer to Lapham was final. She would not sell out, at any price, without the consent of Wunpost. Lapham nodded and darted off—he was a man who dealt with facts and not with the moonshine of sentiment—and this time he fairly flew at Dusty Rhodes. He took him off to one side, where no one could listen in, and at the end of half an hour Mr. Rhodes had signed a paper giving a quit-claim to his interest in the mine. Old Whiskers was summoned from his attendance on the bottles, the lawyer presented his case; and, whatever the arguments, they prevailed also with the saloon-keeper, who signed up and took his check. Presumably they had to do with threats of expensive litigation and appeals to the higher courts, with a learned exposition of the weakness of their case and the air-tight position of Judson Eells; the point is, they prevailed, and Eells took possession of the mine, placing Pisenface Lynch in charge.

Old Whiskers folded his tent and returned to Blackwater, where many of the stampeders had preceded him; and Dusty Rhodes, with a guilty grin, folded his check and started for the railroad. Cole Campbell and his daughter, when they heard the news and found themselves debarred from the property, packed up and took the trail home, and when John C. Calhoun came out of his coma he was left without a friend in the world. The rush had passed on, across the Sink to Blackwater and to the gulches in the mountains beyond; for the men from Nevada had not been slow to comprehend that the Willie Meena held no promise for them.

It was a single rich blow-out in a country otherwise barren; and the tales of the pocket-miners, who held claims back of Blackwater, had led to a second stampede. The Willie Meena was a prophecy of what might be expected if a similar formation could be found, but it was no more than the throat of an extinct volcano, filled up with gold-bearing quartz. There was no fissure-vein, no great mother lode leading off through the country for miles; only a hogback of black quartz and then worlds and worlds of desert as

79

barren as wash boulders could make it. So they rose and went on, like birds in full flight after they have settled for a moment on the plain, and when Wunpost rose up and rubbed his eyes his great camp had passed away like a dream.

Two days later he walked wearily across the desert from Blackwater, with a two gallon canteen under his arm, and at the entrance to Jail Canyon he paused and looked in doubtfully before he shambled up to the house. He was broke, and he knew it, and added to that shame was the greater shame that comes from drink. Old Whiskers' poisonous whiskey had sapped his self-respect, and yet he came on boldly. There was a fever in his eye like that of the gambler who has lost all, yet still watches the fall of the cards; and as Wilhelmina came out he winked at her mysteriously and beckoned her away from the house.

"I've got something good," he told her confidentially; "can you get off to go down to Blackwater?"

"Why, I might," she said. "Father's working up the canyon. Is it something about the mine?"

"Yes, it is," he answered. "Say, what d'ye think of Dusty? He sold us out for five thousand dollars! Five thousand—that's all—and Old Whiskers took the same, giving Judson Eells full control. They cleaned us, Billy, but we'll get our cut yet—do you know what they're trying to do?

Eells is going to organize a company and sell a few shares in order to finance the mine; and if we want to, kid, we can turn in our third interest and get the pro rata in stock. We might as well do it, because they've got the control and otherwise we won't get anything. They've barred us off the property and we'll never get a cent if it produces a million dollars. But look, here's the idea— Judson Eells is badly bent on account of what he lost at Wunpost, and he's crazy to organize a company and market the treasury stock. We'll go in with him, see, and as soon as we get our stock we'll peddle it for what we can get. That'll net us a few thousand and you can take your share and help the old man build his road."

The stubborn look on Billy's face suddenly gave place to one of doubt and then to one of swift decision.

"I'll do it," she said. "We don't need to see Father—just tell them that I've agreed. And when the time comes, send an Indian up to notify me and I'll ride down and sign the papers."

"Good enough!" exclaimed Wunpost with a hint of his old smile. "I'll come up and tell you myself. Have you heard the news from below? Well, every house in Blackwater is plumb full of boomers—and them pocket-miners are all selling out. The whole country's staked, clean back to the peaks, and old Eells says he's going to start a bank. There's three new saloons, a couple more restaurants, and she sure looks like a good live camp—and me, the man that started it and made the whole country, I can't even bum a drink!"

"I'm glad of it," returned Billy, and regarded him so intently that he hastened to change the subject.

"But you wait!" he thundered. "I'll show 'em who's who! I ain't down, by no manner of means. I've got a mine or two hid out that would make 'em fairly scream if I'd show 'em a piece of the rock. All I need is a little capital, just a few thousand dollars to get me a good outfit of mules, and I'll come back into Blackwater with a pack-load of ore that'll make 'em *all* sit up and take notice."

He swung his fist into his hand with oratorical fervor and Mrs. Campbell appeared suddenly at the door. Her first favorable impression of the gallant young Southerner had been changed by the course of events and she was now morally certain that the envious Dusty Rhodes had come nearer the unvarnished truth. To be sure he had apologized, but Wunpost himself had said that it was only to gain a share in the mine—and how lamentably had Wunpost failed, after all his windy boasts, when it came to a conflict with Judson Eells. He had weakened like a schoolboy, all his arguments had been puerile; and even her husband, who was far from censorious, had stated that the whole affair was badly handled.

And now here he was, after a secret conference with her daughter, suddenly bursting into vehement protestations and hinting at still other hidden mines. Well, his mines might be as rich as he declared them to be, but Mrs. Campbell herself was dubious.

"Wilhelmina," she called, "don't stand out in the sun! Why don't you invite Mr. Calhoun to the house?"

The hint was sufficient, Mr. Calhoun excused himself hastily and went striding away down the canyon; and Wilhelmina, after a perfunctory return to the house, slipped out and ran up to her lookout. Not a word that he had said about the rush to Blackwater was in any way startling to her; she had seen every dust-cloud, marked each automobile as it rushed past, and even noted the stampede from the west. For the natural way to Blackwater was not across Death Valley from the distant Nevada camps, but from the railroad which lay only forty miles to the west and was reached by an automobile stage. The road came down through Sheep-herder Canyon, on the other side of the Sink, and every day as she looked across its vastness she saw the long trailers of dust. She knew that the autos were rushing in with men and the slow freighters were hauling in supplies—all the real news for her was the number of saloons and restaurants, and that Eells was starting a bank.

A bank! And in Blackwater! The only bank that Blackwater had ever had or needed was the safe in Old Whiskers' saloon; and now this rich schemer, this iron-handed robber, was going to start a bank! Billy lay inside the portal of her gate of dreams and watched Wunpost as he plodded across the plain, and she resolved to join with him and do her level best to bring Eells' plans to naught. If he was counting on the sale of his treasury stock to fill up the vaults of his bank he would find others in the market with stock in both hands, peddling it out to the highest bidder. And even if the mine was worth into the millions, she, for one, would sell every share. It was best, after all, since Eells owned the control, to sell out for what they could get; and if this was merely a deep-laid scheme to buy in their stock for almost nothing they would at least have a little ready cash.

The Campbells were poor; her father even lacked the money to buy powder to blast out his road, and so he struggled on, grading up the easy places and leaving Corkscrew Gorge untouched. That would call for heavy blasting and crews of hardy men to climb up and shoot down the walls, and even after that the jagged rock-bed must be covered and leveled to the semblance of a road. Now nothing but a trail led up through the dark passageway, where grinding boulders had polished the walls like glass; and until that

84

gateway was opened Cole Campbell's road was useless; it might as well be all trail. But with five thousand dollars, or even less—with whatever she received from her stock—the gateway could be conquered, her father's dream would come true and all their life would be changed.

There would be a road, right past their house, where great trucks would lumber forth loaded down with ore from their mine, and return ladened with machinery from the railroad. There would be miners going by and stopping for a drink, and someone to talk to every day, and the loneliness which oppressed her like a physical pain would give place to gaiety and peace. Her father would be happy and stop working so hard, and her mother would not have to worry—all if she, Wilhelmina, could just sell her stock and salvage a pittance from the wreck.

She knew now what Wunpost had meant when he had described the outside world and the men they would meet at the rush, yet for all his hard-won knowledge he had gone down once more before Judson Eells and his gang. But he had spoken true when he said they would resort to murder to gain possession of their mine, and though he had yielded at last to the lure of strong drink, in her heart she could not blame him too much. It was not by wrongdoing that he had wrecked their high hopes, but by signing a contract long years before without reading what he called the fine print. He was just a boy, after all, in spite of his boasting and his vaunted knowledge of the world; and now in his trouble he had come back to her, to the one person he knew he could trust. She gazed a long time at the dwindling form till it was lost in the immensity of the plain; and then she gazed on, for dreams were all she had to comfort her lonely heart.

CHAPTER VIII

THE BABES IN THE WOODS

EVER since David went forth and slew Goliath with his sling, youth has set its puny lance to strike down giants; and history, making much of the hotspurs who won, draws a veil over the striplings who were slain. And yet all who know the stern conditions of life must recognize that youth is a handicap, and if David had but donned the heavy armor of King Saul he too would have gone to his death. But instead he stepped forth untrammeled by its weight, with nothing but a stone and a sling, and because the scoffing giant refused to raise his shield he was struck down by the pebble of a child. But giant Judson Eells was in a baby-killing mood when he invited Wunpost and Wilhelmina to his den; and when they emerged, after signing articles of incorporation, he licked his chops and smiled.

It developed at the meeting that the sole function of a stockholder is to vote for the Directors of the Company; and, having elected Eells and Lapham and John C. Calhoun Directors, the stockholders' meeting adjourned. Reconvening immediately as a Board of Directors, Judson Eells was elected President, John C. Calhoun, Vice-President and Phillip F.

Lapham Secretary-treasurer—after which an assessment of ten cents a share was levied upon all the stock. Exit John C. Calhoun and Wilhelmina Campbell, stripped of their stock and all faith in mankind. For even if by some miracle they should raise the necessary sum Judson Eells and Phillip Lapham would immediately vote a second assessment, and so on, *ad infinitum.* Holding a majority of the stock, Eells could control the Board of Directors, and through it the policies of the company; and any assessments which he himself might pay would but be transferred from one pocket to the other. It was as neat a job of baby-killing as Eells had ever accomplished, and he slew them both with a smile.

They had conspired in their innocence to gain stock in the company and to hawk it about the streets; but neither had thought to suggest the customary Article: "The stock of said company shall be non-assessable." The Articles of Incorporation had been drawn up by Phillip F. Lapham; and yet, after all his hard experiences, Wunpost was so awed by the legal procedure that he forgot all about the fine print. Not that it made any difference, they would have trimmed him anyway, but it was three times in the very same place! He cursed himself out loud for an ignorant baboon and left Wilhelmina in tears.

She had come down with her mother, her

father being busy, and they had planned to take in the town; but after this final misfortune Wilhelmina lost all interest in the busy marts of trade. What to her were clothes and shoes when she had no money to buy them—and when overdressed women, none too chaste in their demeanor, stared after her in boorish amusement? Blackwater had become a great city, but it was not for her—the empty honor of having the Willie Meena named after her was all she had won from her mine. John C. Calhoun had been right when he warned her, long before, that the mining game was more like a dog fight than it was like a Sunday school picnic; and yet— well, some people made money at it. Perhaps they were better at reading the fine print, and not so precipitate about signing Articles of Incorporation, but as far as she was concerned Wilhelmina made a vow never to trust a lawyer again.

She returned to the ranch, where the neglected garden soon showed signs of her changing mood; but after the weeds had been chopped out and routed she slipped back to her lookout on the hill. It was easier to tear the weeds from a tangled garden than old memories from her lonely heart; and she took up, against her will, the old watch for Wunpost, who had departed from Blackwater in a fury. He had stood on the corner and, oblivious of her presence, had poured out the vials of his wrath; he had cursed Eells for a swindler, and Lapham for his dog and Lynch for his yellow hound. He had challenged them all, either individually or collectively, to come forth and meet him in battle; and then he had offered to fight any man in Blackwater who would say a good word for any of them. But Blackwater looked on in cynical amusement, for Eells was the making of the town; and when he had given off the worst of his venom Wunpost had tied up his roll and departed.

He had left as he had come, a single-blanket tourist, packing his worldly possessions on his back; and when last seen by Wilhelmina he was headed east, up the wash that came down from the Panamints. Where he was going, when he would return, if he ever would return, all were mysteries to the girl who waited on; and if she watched for him it was because there was no one else whose coming would stir her heart. Far up the canyon and over the divide there lived Hungry Bill and his family, but Hungry was an Indian and when he dropped in it was always to get something to eat. He had two sons and two daughters, whom he kept enslaved, forbidding them to even think of marriage; and all his thoughts were of money and things to eat, for Hungry Bill was an Indian miser.

He came through often now with his burros packed with fruit from the abandoned whiteman's ranch that he had occupied; and even his wild-eyed daughters had more variety than Billy, for they accompanied him to Blackwater and Willie Meena. There they sold their grapes and peaches at exorbitant prices and came back with coffee and flour, but neither would say a word for fear of their old father, who watched them with intolerant eyes. They were evil, snaky eyes, for it was said that in his day he had waylaid many a venturesome prospector, and while they gleamed ingratiatingly when he was presented with food, at no time did they show good will. He was still a renegade at heart, shunned and avoided by his own kinsmen, the Shoshones who camped around Wild Rose; but it was from him, from this old tyrant that she despised so cordially, that Wilhelmina received her first news of Wunpost.

Hungry Bill came up grinning, on his way down from his ranch, and fixed her with his glittering black eyes.

"You savvy Wunpo?" he asked, "hi-ko man—*busca* gol'? Him sendum piece of lock!"

He produced a piece of rock from a knot in his shirt-tail and handed it over to her slowly. It was a small chunk of polished quartz, half green, half turquoise blue; and in the center, like a jewel, a crystal of yellow gold gleamed out from its matrix of blue. Wilhelmina gazed at it blankly, then flushed and turned away as she felt Hungry

91

Bill's eyes upon her. He was a disreputable old wretch, who imputed to others the base motives which governed his own acts; and when she read his black heart Wilhelmina straightened up and gave him back the stone.

"No, you keepum!" protested Hungry. "Hi-ko ketchum plenty mo'."

But Wilhelmina shook her head.

"No!" she said, "you give that to my mother. Are those your girls down there? Well, why don't you let them come up to the house? You no good—I don't like bad Indians!"

She turned away from him, still frowning angrily, and strode on down to the creek; but the daughters of Hungry Bill, in their groveling way, seemed to share the low ideals of their father. They were tall and sturdy girls, clad in breezy calico dresses and with their hair down over their eyes; and as they gazed out from beneath their bangs a guilty smile contorted their lips, a smile that made Wilhelmina writhe.

"What's the matter with you?" she snapped, and as the scared look came back she turned on her heel and left them. What could one expect, of course, from Hungry Bill's daughters after they had been guarded like the slave-girls in a harem; but the joy of hearing from Wunpost was quite lost in the fierce anger which the conduct of his messengers evoked. He was up there, somewhere, and he had made another strike—the most beautiful blue quartz in the world—but these renegade Shoshones with their understanding smiles had quite killed the pleasure of it for her. She returned to the house where Hungry Bill, in the kitchen, was wolfing down a great pan of beans; but the sight of the old glutton with his mouth down to the plate quite sickened her and drove her away. Wunpost was up in the hills, and he had made a strike, but with that she must remain content until he either came down himself or chose a more high-minded messenger.

Hungry Bill went on to Blackwater and came back with a load of supplies, which he claimed he was taking to "Wunpo"; and, after he had passed up the canyon, Wilhelmina strolled along behind him. At the mouth of Corkscrew Gorge there was a great pool of water, overshadowed by a rank growth of willows through whose tops the wild grapevines ran riot. Here it had been her custom, during the heat of the day, to paddle along the shallows or sit and enjoy the cool air. There was always a breeze at the mouth of Corkscrew Gorge, and when it drew down, as it did on this day, it carried the odors of dank caverns. In the dark and gloomy depths of this gash through the hills the rocks were always damp and cold; and beneath the great waterfalls, where the cloudbursts had scooped out pot-holes, there was a delicious mist and spray. She dawdled by the willows, then splashed on up the slippery trail until, above the last echoing waterfall, she stepped out into the world beyond.

The great canyon spread out again, once she had passed the waterworn Gorge, and peak after peak rose up to right and left where yawning side canyons led in. But all were set on edge and reared up to dizzying heights; and along their scarred flanks there lay huge slides of shaley rock, ready to slip at the touch of a hand. Vivid stripes of red and green, alternating with layers of blue and white, painted the sides of the striated ridges; and odd seams here and there showed dull yellows and chocolate browns like the edge of a crumbled layer-cake. Up the canyon the walls shut in again, and then they opened out, and so on for nine miles until Old Panamint was reached and the open valley sloped up to the summit.

Many a time in the old days when they had lived in Panamint had Wilhelmina scaled those far heights; the huge white wall of granite dotted with ball-like piñons and junipers, which fenced them from Death Valley beyond. It opened up like a gulf, once the summit was reached, and below the jagged precipices stretched long ridges and fan-like washes which lost themselves at last in the Sink. For a hundred miles to the north and the south it lay, a writhing ribbon of white, pinching down to narrow strips, then broadening out in gleaming marshes; and on both sides the mountains rose up black and forbidding, a bulwark against the sky. Wilhelmina had never entered it, she had been content to look down; and then she crept back to beautiful sheltered Panamint where father had his mine.

It was up on the ridge, where the white granite of the summit came into contact with the burnt limestone and schist; and, of all the rich mines, the Homestake was the best, until the cloudburst came along and spoiled all of them. Wilhelmina still remembered how the great flood had passed the town, moving boulders as if they were pebbles; but not until it reached the place where she stood had it done irretrievable damage. The roadbed was washed out, but the streambed remained, and the banks from which to fill in more dirt; but when the flood struck the Gorge it backed up into a lake, for the narrow defile was choked. Trees and rocks and rumbling boulders had piled up against its entrance, holding the waters back like a dam; and when they broke through they sluiced everything before them, gouging the canyon down to the bed-rock. Now twelve years had passed by and only a hazardous trail threaded the Gorge which had once been a highway.

Wilhelmina gazed up the valley and sighed again, for since that terrific cloudburst she had been stranded in Jail Canyon like a piece of driftwood tossed up by the flood. Nothing happened to her, any more than to the piñon logs which the waters had wedged high above the stream, and as she returned home down the Gorge she almost wished for another flood, to float them and herself away. No one came by there any more, the trail was so poor, and yet her father still clung to the mine; but a flood would either fill up the Gorge with débris or make even him give up hope. She sank down by the cool pool and put her feet in the water, dabbling them about like a wilful child; but at a shout from below she rose up a grown woman, for she knew it was Dusty Rhodes.

He came on up the creek-bed with his burros on the trot, hurling clubs at the laggards as he ran; and when they stopped short at the sight of Wilhelmina he almost rushed them over her. But a burro is a creature of lively imagination, to whom the unknown is always terrible; and at a fresh outburst from Dusty the whole outfit took to the brush, leaving him face to face with his erstwhile partner.

"Oh, hello, hello!" he called out gruffly. "Say, did Hungry Bill go through here? He was jest down to Blackwater, buying some grub at the store, and he paid for it with rock that was *half gold!* So git out of the road, my little girl—I'm going up to prospect them hills!"

"Don't you call me your little girl!" called back

96

Billy angrily. "And Hungry Bill hasn't got any mine!"

"Oh, he ain't, hey?" mocked Dusty, leaving his burros to browse while he strode triumphantly up to her. "Then jest look at *that,* my—my fine young lady! I got it from the store-keeper myself!"

He handed her a piece of green and blue quartz, but she only glanced at it languidly. The memory of his perfidy on a previous occasion made her long to puncture his pride, and she passed the gold ore back to him.

"I've seen that before," she said with a sniff, "so you can stop driving those burros so hard. It came from Wunpost's mine."

"Wunpost!" yelled Dusty Rhodes, his eyes getting big; and then he spat out an oath. "Who told ye?" he demanded, sticking his face into hers, and she stepped away disdainfully.

"Hungry Bill," she said, and watched him writhe as the bitter truth went home. "You think you're so smart," she taunted at last, "why don't you go out and find one for yourself? I suppose you want to rush in and claim a half interest in his strike and then sell out to old Eells. I hope he kills you, if you try to do it—*I* would, if I were him. What'd you do with that five thousand dollars?"

"Eh—eh—that's none of your business," bleated Dusty Rhodes, whose trip to Los Angeles

97

had proved disastrous. "And if Wunpost gave Hungry that sack of ore he stole it from some other feller's mine. I knowed all along he'd locate that Black P'int if I ever let him stop—I've had my eye on it for years—and that's why I hurried by. I discovered it myself, only I never told nobody—he must have heard me talking in my sleep!"

"Yes, or when you were drunk!" suggested Wilhelmina maliciously. "I hear you got robbed in Los Angeles. And anyhow I'm glad, because you stole that five thousand dollars, and no good ever came from stolen property."

"Oh, it didn't, hey?" sneered Dusty, who was recovering his poise, "well, I'll bet ye *this* rock was stolen! And if that's the case, where does your young man git off, that you think the world and all of? But you've got to show me that he ever *saw* this rock—I believe old Hungry was lying to you!"

"Well, don't let me keep you!" cried Billy, bowing mockingly. "Go on over and ask him yourself—but I'll bet you don't *dare* to meet Wunpost!"

"How come Hungry to tell you?" burst out Dusty Rhodes at last, and Wilhelmina smiled mysteriously.

"That's none of your business, my busy little man," she mimicked in patronizing tones, "but I've got a piece of that rock right up at the house.

98

You go back there and mother will show it to you."

"I'm going on!" answered Dusty with instant decision; "can't stop to make no visit today. They's a big rush coming—every burro-man in Blackwater—and some of them are legging it afoot. But that thieving son of a goat, *he* never found no mine! I know it—it can't be possible!"

CHAPTER IX

A NEW DEAL

THE rush of burro-men to Hungry Bill's ranch followed close in Dusty Rhodes' wake, and some there were who came on foot; but they soon came stringing back, for it was a fine, large country and Hungry Bill was about as communicative as a rattlesnake. All he knew, or cared to know, was the price of corn and fruit, which he sold at Blackwater prices; and the search for Wunpost had only served to show to what lengths a man will go for revenge. In some mysterious way Wunpost had acquired a horse and mule, both sharp-shod for climbing over rocks, and he had dallied at Hungry Bill's until the first of the stampeders had come in sight on the Panamint trail. Then he had set out up the ridge, riding the horse and packing the mule, and even an Indian trailer had given out and quit without ever bringing them in sight of him again. He had led them such a chase that the hardiest came back satisfied, and they agreed that he could keep his old mine.

The excitement died away or was diverted to other channels, for Blackwater was having a boom; and, just as Wilhelmina had given up hope of seeing him, John C. Calhoun came riding down the ridge. Not down the canyon, where the trail made riding easy, but down the steep ridge trail, where a band of mountain sheep was accustomed to come for water. Wilhelmina was in her tunnel, looking down with envious eyes at the traffic in the valley below; and he came upon her suddenly, so suddenly it made her jump, for no one ever rode up there.

"Hello!" he hailed, spurring his horse up to the portal and letting out his rope as he entered. "Kinder hot, out there in the sun. Well, how's tricks?" he inquired, sitting down in the shade and wiping the streaming sweat from his eyes. "Hungry Bill says you s-spurned my gold!"

"What did you tell that old Indian?" burst out Wilhelmina wrathfully, and Wunpost looked up in surprise.

"Why, nothing," he said, "only to get me some grub and give you that piece of polished rock. How was that for the real old high-grade? From my new mine, up in the high country. What's the matter—did Hungry get gay?"

"Well—not that," hesitated Wilhelmina, "but he looked at me so funny that I told him to give it to Mother. What was it you told him about me?"

"Not a thing," protested Wunpost, "just to give you the rock. Oh, I know!" He laughed and slapped his leg. "He's scared some prospector will steal one of them gals, and I told him not to worry about *me*. Guess that gave him a tip, because he looked wise as a prairie dog when I told him to give that specimen to you." He paused and knocked the dust out of his battered old hat, then glanced up from under his eyebrows.

"Ain't mad, are you?" he asked, "because if you are I'm on my way—"

"Oh, no!" she answered quickly. "Where have you been all the time? Dusty Rhodes came through here, looking for you."

"Yes, they all came," he grinned, "but I showed 'em some sheep-trails before they got tired of chasing me. I knew for a certainty that those mugs would follow Hungry—they did the same thing over in Nevada. I sent in an Indian to buy me a little grub and they trailed me clean across Death Valley. Guess that ore must have looked pretty good."

"Where'd you get it?" she asked, and he rolled his eyes roguishly while a crafty smile lit up his face.

"That's a question," he said. "If I'd tell you, you'd have the answer. But I'm not going to show it to *nobody!*"

"Well, you don't need to think that *I* care!" she spoke up resentfully, "nobody asked you to show them your gold. And after what happened with the Willie Meena I wouldn't take your old mine for a gift."

"You won't have to," he replied. "I've quit taking in pardners—it's a lone hand for me, after this. I'm sure slow in the head, but I reckon I've learned my lesson—never go up against the other man's game. Old Eells is a lawyer and I tried to beat him at law. We've switched the deal now and he can play *my* game a while—hide-and-seek, up in them high peaks."

He waved his hand in the direction of the Panamints and winked at her exultantly.

"Look at *that!*" he said, and drew a rock from his shirt pocket which was caked and studded with gold. It was more like a chunk of gold with a little quartz attached to it, and as she exclaimed he leaned back and gloated. "I've got worlds of it!" he declared. "Let 'em get out and rustle for it—that's the way I made my start. By the time they've rode as far as I have they'll know she's a mountain sheep country. I located two mines right smack beside the trail and these jaspers came along and stole them both. All right! Fine! Fine! Let 'em look for the old Sockdolager where I got this gold, and the first man that finds it can have it! I'm a sport—I haven't even staked it!"

"And can *I* have it?" asked Billy, her eyes beginning to glow, "because, oh, we need money so bad!"

"What for, kid?" inquired Wunpost with a fatherly smile. "Ain't you got a good home, and everything?"

"Yes, but the road—Father's road. If I just had the money we'd start right in on it tomorrow."

"Hoo! I'll build you the road!" declared Wunpost munificently. "And it won't cost either one of us a cent. Don't believe it, eh? You think this is bunk? Then I'll tell you, kid, what I'll do. I'll make you a bet we'll have a wagon-road up that canyon before three months are up. And all by head-work, mind ye—not a dollar of our own money—might even get old Eells to build it. Yes, I'm serious; I've got a new system—been thinking it out, up in the hills—and just to show you how brainy I am I'll make this demonstration for nothing. You don't need to bet me anything, just acknowledge that I'm the king when it comes to the real inside work; and before I get through I'll have Judson Eells belly up and gasping for air like a fish. I'm going to trim him, the big fat slob; I'm going to give him a lesson that'll learn him to lay off of me for life; I'm going to make him so scared he'll step down into the gutter when he meets me coming down the sidewalk. Well, laugh, doggone it, but you watch my dust—I'm going to hang his hide on the fence!"

"That's what you told me before," she reminded him mischievously, "but somehow it didn't work out."

"It'll work out this time," he retorted grimly. "A man has got to learn. I'm just a kid, I know that, and I'm not much on book learning, but don't you never say I can't *think!* Maybe I can't beat them crooks when I play their own game, but this time *I deal the hand!* Do you git me? We've switched the deal! And if I don't ring in a cold deck and deal from the bottom it won't be because it's *wrong.* I'm out to scalp 'em, see, and just to convince you we'll begin by building that road. Your old man is wrong, he don't need no road and it won't do him any good when he gets it; but just to make you happy and show you how much I think of you, I'll do it—only you've got to stand pat! No Sunday school stuff, see? We're going to fight this out with hay hooks, and when I come back with his hair don't blame *me* if old Eells makes a roar. I'm going to stick him, see; and I'm not going to stick him once—I'm going to stick him three times, till he squeals like a pig, because that's what he did to me! He cleaned me once on the Wunpost, and twice on the Willie Meena, but before I get through with him he'll knock a corner off the mountain every time he sees my dust. He'll be *gone,* you understand—it'll be moving day for him—but I'll chase him to the hottest stope in hell. I'm going to bust him, savvy, just to learn these other dastards not to start any rough stuff with me. And now the road, the road! We'll just get him to build it— I've got it all framed up!"

He made a bluff to kiss her, then ran out and mounted his horse and went rollicking off towards Blackwater. Wilhelmina brushed her cheek and gazed angrily after him, then smiled and turned away with a sigh.

CHAPTER X

THE SHORT SPORTS

THE booming mining camp of Blackwater stood under the rim of a high mesa, between it and an alkali flat, and as Wunpost rode in he looked it over critically, though with none too friendly eyes. Being laid out in a land of magnificent distances, there was plenty of room between the houses, and the broad main street seemed more suited for driving cattle than for accommodating the scant local traffic. There had been a time when all that space was needed to give swing-room to twenty-mule teams, but that time was past and the two sparse rows of houses seemed dwarfed and pitifully few. Yet there were new ones going up, and quite a sprinkling of tents; and down on the corner Wunpost saw a big building which he knew must be Judson Eells' bank.

It had sprung up in his absence, a pretentious structure of solid concrete, and as he jogged along past it Wunpost swung his head and looked it over scornfully. The walls were thick and strong, but that was no great credit, for in that desert country any man who would get water could mix concrete until he was tired. All in the world he had to do was to scoop up the ground and pour the mud into the molds, and when it was set he had a natural concrete, composed of lime and coarse gravel and bone-dry dust. Half the burro-corrals in Blackwater were built out of concrete, but Eells had put up a big false front. This had run into money, the ornately stamped tin-work having been shipped all the way from Los Angeles; and there were two plate-glass windows that framed a passing view of marble pillars and shining brass grilles. Wunpost took it all in and then hissed through his teeth—the money that had built it was his!

"I'll skin him!" he muttered, and pulled up down the street before Old Whiskers' populous saloon. Several men drifted out to speak to him as he tied his horse and pack, but he greeted them all with such a venomous glare that they shied off and went across the street. There there stood a rival saloon, rushed up in Wunpost's absence; but after looking it over he went into Whiskers' Place, which immediately began to fill up. The coming of Wunpost had been noted from afar, and a man who buys his grub with jewelry gold-specimens is sure to have a following. He slouched in sulkily and gazed at Old Whiskers, who was chewing on his tobacco like a ruminative billygoat and pretending to polish the bar. It was borne in on Whiskers that he had refused Wunpost a drink on the day he had walked out of camp, but he was hoping that the slight was forgotten; for if he could keep him in his saloon all the others would soon be vacated, now that Wunpost was the talk of the town. He had found one mine and lost it and gone out and found another one while the rest of them were wearing out shoe-leather; and a man like that could not be ignored by the community, no matter if he did curse their town. So Whiskers chewed on, not daring to claim his friendship, and Wunpost leaned against the bar.

"Gimme a drink," he said laying fifteen cents before him; and as several men moved forward he scowled at them in silence and tossed off his *solamente.* "Cr-ripes!" he shuddered, "did you make that yourself?" And when Whiskers, caught unawares, half acquiesced, Wunpost drew himself up and burst forth. "I believe it!" he announced with an oracular nod, "I can taste the burnt sugar, the fusel oil, the wood alcohol and everything. One drink of that stuff would strike a stone Injun blind if it wasn't for this dry desert air. They tell me, Whiskers, that when you came to this town you brought one barrel of whiskey with you—and that you ain't ordered another one since. That stuff is all right for those that like it—I'm going across the street."

He strode out the door, taking the fickle crowd with him and leaving Old Whiskers to chew the cud of brooding bitterness. In the saloon across the street a city barkeeper greeted Wunpost affably, and inquired what it would be. Wunpost asked for a drink and the discerning barkeeper set out a bottle with the seal uncut. It was bonded goods, guaranteed seven years in the wood, and Wunpost smacked his lips as he tasted it.

"Have one yourself," he suggested and while the crowd stood agape he laid down a nugget of gold.

That settled it with Blackwater, they threw their money on the bar and tried to get him drunk, but Wunpost would drink with none of them.

"No, you bunch of bootlickers!" he shouted angrily, "go on away, I won't have nothing to do with you! When I was broke you wouldn't treat me and now that I'm flush I reckon I can buy my own liquor. You're all sucking around old Eells, saying he made the town—I made your danged town myself! Didn't I discover the Willie Meena—and ain't that what made the town? Well, go chase yourselves, you suckers, I'm through with ye! You did me dirt when you thought I was cleaned and now you can all go to blazes!"

He shook hands with the friendly barkeeper, told him to keep the change, and fought his way out to the street. The crowd of boomers, still refusing to be insulted, trooped shamelessly along in his wake; and when he unpacked his mule and took out two heavy, heavy ore-sacks

110

even Judson Eells cast aside his dignity. He had looked on from afar, standing in front of the plate-glass window which had "Willie Meena Mining Company" across it; but at a signal from Lynch, who had been acting as his lookout, he came running to demand his rights. The acquisition of the Wunpost and the Willie Meena properties had by no means satisfied his lust; and since this one crazy prospector—who of all men he had grubstaked seemed the only one who could find a mine—had for the third time come in with rich ore, he felt no compunctions about claiming his share.

"Where'd you get that ore?" he demanded of Wunpost as the crowd opened up before him and Wunpost glanced at him fleeringly.

"I stole it!" he said and went on sorting out specimens which he stuffed into his well-worn overalls.

"I asked you *where!*" returned Eells, drawing his lip up sternly, and Wunpost turned to the crowd.

"You see?" he jeered, "I told you he was crooked. He wants to go and steal some himself." He laughed, long and loud, and some there were who joined in with him, for Eells was not without his enemies. To be sure he had built the bank, and established his offices in Blackwater when he might have started a new town at the mine; but no moneylender was ever universally popular and Eells was ruthless in exacting his usury. But on the other hand he had brought a world of money in to town, for the Willie Meena had paid from the first; and it was his pay-roll and the wealth which had followed in his wake that had made the camp what it was; so no one laughed as long or as loud as John C. Calhoun and he hunched his shoulders and quit.

"Never you mind where I stole it!" he said to Eells, "I stole it, and that's enough. Is there anything in your contract that gives you a cut on everything I *steal?*"

"Why—why, no," replied Eells, "but that isn't the point—I asked you where you got it. If it's stolen, that's one thing, but if you've located another mine—"

"I haven't!" put in Wunpost, "you've broke me of that. The only way I can keep anything now is to steal it. Because, no matter what it is, if I come by it honestly, you and your rabbit-faced lawyer will grab it; but if I go out and steal it you don't dare to claim half, because that would make you out a thief. And of course a banker, and a big mining magnate, and the owner of the famous Willie Meena—well, it just isn't done, that's all."

He twisted up his lips in a wry, sarcastic smile but Eells was not susceptible to irony. He was the bulldog type of man, the kind that takes hold and hangs on, and he could see that the ore was rich. It was so rich indeed that in those two sacks

112

alone there were undoubtedly several thousand dollars—and the mine itself might be worth millions. Eells turned and beckoned to Phillip F. Lapham, who was looking on with greedy eyes. They consulted together while Wunpost waited calmly, though with the battle light in his eyes, and at last Eells returned to the charge.

"Mr. Calhoun," he said, "there's no use to pretend that this ore which you have is stolen. We have seen samples of it before and it is very unusual—in fact, no one has seen anything like it. Therefore your claim that it is stolen is a palpable pretense, to deprive me of my rights under our constitution."

"Yes?" prompted Wunpost, dropping his hand on his pistol, and Eells paused and glanced at Lapham.

"Well," he conceded, "of course I can't prove anything and—"

"No, you bet you can't prove anything," spoke up Wunpost defiantly, "and you can't touch an ounce of my ore. It's mine and I stole it and no court can make me show where; because a man can't be compelled to incriminate himself—and if I showed you they could come out and pinch me. Huh! You've got a lawyer, have you? Well, I've got one myself and I know my legal rights and if any man puts out his hand to take away this bag, I've got a right to shoot him dead! Ain't that right now, Mr. Flip Flappum?"

113

"Well—the law gives one the right to defend his own property; but only with sufficient force to resist the attack, and to shoot would be excessive."

"Not with me!" asserted Wunpost, "I've consulted one of the best lawyers in Nevada and I'm posted on every detail. There's Pisen-face Lynch, that everybody knows is a gun-man in the employ of Judson Eells, and at the first crooked move I'd be justified in killing him and then in killing you and Eells. Oh, I'll law you, you dastards, I'll law you with a six-shooter—and I've got an attorney all hired to defend me. We've agreed on his fee and I've got it all buried where he can go get it when I give him the directions; and I hope he gets it soon because then there'll be just three less grafters, to rob honest prospectors of their rights."

He advanced upon Lapham, his great head thrust out as he followed his squirming flight through the crowd; and when he was gone he turned upon Eells who stood his ground with insolent courage.

"And you, you big slob," he went on threateningly, "you don't need to think you'll git off. I ain't afraid of your gun-man, and I ain't afraid of you, and before we get through I'm going to *git* you. Well, laugh if you want to—it's your scalp or mine—and you can jest politely go to hell."

114

He snapped his fingers in his face and, taking a sack in both hands, started off to the Wells Fargo office; and, so intimidated for once were Eells and his gun-fighter, that neither one followed along after him. Wunpost deposited his treasure in the Express Company's safe and went off to care for his animals and, while the crowd dispersed to the several saloons, Eells and Lapham went into conference. This sudden glib quoting of moot points of law was a new and disturbing factor, and Lapham himself was quite unstrung over the news of the buried retainer. It had all the earmarks of a criminal lawyer's work, this tender solicitude for his fee; and some shysters that Lapham knew would even encourage their client to violence, if it would bring them any nearer to the gold. But this gold—where did it come from? Could it possibly be high-graded, in spite of all the testimony to the contrary? And if not, if his claim that it was stolen was a blind, then how could they discover its whereabouts? Certainly not by force of law, and not by any violence—they must resort to guile, the old cunning of the serpent, which now differentiates man from the beasts of the field, and perhaps they could get Wunpost drunk!

Happy thought! The wires were laid and all Blackwater joined in with them, in fact it was the universal idea, and even the new barkeeper with whom Wunpost had struck up an acquaintance

115

had promised to do his part. To get Wunpost drunk and then to make him boast, to pique him by professed doubts of his great find; and then when he spilled it, as he had always done before, the wild rush and another great boom! They watched his every move as he put his animals in a corral and stored his packs and saddles; and when, in the evening, he drifted back to The Mint, man after man tried to buy him a drink. But Wunpost was antisocial, he would have none of their whiskey and their canting professions of friendship; only Ben Fellowes, the new barkeeper, was good enough for his society and he joined him in several libations. It was all case goods, very soft and smooth and velvety, and yet in a remarkably short space of time Wunpost was observed to be getting garrulous.

"I'll tell you, pardner," he said taking the barkeeper by the arm and speaking very confidently into his ear, "I'll tell you, it's this way with me. I'm a Calhoun, see—John C. Calhoun is my name, and I come from the state of Kentucky—and a Kentucky Calhoun never forgets a friend, and he never forgets an enemy. I'm burned out on this town—don't like it— nothing about it—but you, now, you're different, you never done me any injury. You're my friend, ain't that right, you're my friend!"

The barkeeper reassured him and held his breath while he poured out another drink and then, as Wunpost renewed his protestations, Fellowes thanked him for his present of the nugget.

"What—*that?*" exclaimed Wunpost brushing the piece of gold aside, "that's nothing—here, give you a good one!" He drew out a chunk of rock fairly encrusted with gold and forced it roughly upon him. "It's nothing!" he said, "lots more where that came from. Got system, see—know how to find it. All these water-hole prospectors, they never find nothing—too lazy, won't get out and hunt. I head for the high places—leap from crag to crag, see, like mountain sheep—come back with my pockets full of gold. These bums are no good—I could take 'em out tonight and lead 'em to my mine and they'd never be able to go back. Rough country 'n all that—no trails, steep as the devil—take 'em out there and lose 'em, every time. Take you out and lose you—now say, you're my friend, I'll tell you what I'll do."

He stopped with portentous dignity and poured out another drink and the barkeeper frowned a hanger-on away.

"I'll take you out there," went on Wunpost, "and show you my mine—show you the place where I get all this gold. You can pick up all you want, and when we get back you give me a thousand dollar bill. That's all I ask is a thousand dollar bill—like to have one to flash on the

117

boys—and then we'll go to Los and blow the whole pile—by grab, I'm a high-roller, right. I'm a good feller, see, as long as you're my friend, but don't tip off this place to old Eells. Have to kill you if you do—he's bad actor—robbed me twice. What's matter—ain't you got the dollar bill?"

"You said a thousand dollars!" spoke up the barkeeper breathlessly.

"Well, thousand dollar bill, then. Ain't you got it—what's the matter? Aw, gimme another drink—you're nothing but a bunch of short sports."

He shook his head and sighed and as the barkeeper began to sweat he caught the hanger-on's eye. It was Pisen-face Lynch and he was winking at him fiercely, meanwhile tapping his own pocket significantly.

"I can get it," ventured the barkeeper but Wunpost ignored him.

"You're all short sports," he asserted drunkenly, waving his hand insultingly at the crowd. "You're cheap guys—you can't bear to lose."

"Hey!" broke in the barkeeper, "I said I'd take you up. I'll get the thousand dollars, all right."

"Oh, you will, eh?" murmured Wunpost and then he shook himself together. "Oh—sure! Yes, all right! Come on, we'll start right now!"

CHAPTER XI

THE STINGING LIZARD

IN a certain stratum of society, now about to become extinct, it is considered quite *au fait* to roll a drunk if circumstances will permit. And it was from this particular stratum that the barkeeper at The Mint had derived his moral concepts. Therefore he considered it no crime, no betrayal of a trust, to borrow the thousand dollars with which he was to pay John C. Calhoun from that prince of opportunists, Judson Eells. It is not every banker that will thrust a thousand dollar bill—and the only one he has on hand—upon a member of the bungstarters' brotherhood; but a word in his ear from Pisen-face Lynch convinced Fellowes that it would be well to run straight. Fate had snatched him from behind the bar to carry out a part not unconnected with certain schemes of Judson Eells and any tendency to run out on his trusting backers would be visited with summary punishment. At least that was what he gathered in the brief moment they had together before Lynch gave him the money and disappeared.

As for John C. Calhoun, a close student of inebriety might have noticed that he became sober too quick; but he invested their departure in such a wealth of mystery that the barkeeper was more than satisfied. A short ways out of town Wunpost turned out into the rocks and milled around for an hour; and then, when their trail was hopelessly lost, he led the way into the hills. Being a stranger in the country Fellowes could not say what wash it was, but they passed up *some* wash and from that into another one; and so on until he was lost; and the most he could do was to drop a few white beans from the pocketful that Lynch had provided. The night was very dark and they rode on interminably, camping at dawn in a shut-in canyon; and so on for three nights until his mind became a blank as far as direction was concerned. His liberal supply of beans had been exhausted the first night and since then they had passed over a hundred rocky hogbacks and down a thousand boulder-strewn canyons. As to the whereabouts of Blackwater he had no more idea than a cat that has been carried in a bag; and he lacked that intimate sense of direction which often enables the cat to come back. He was lost, and a little scared, when Wunpost stopped in a gulch and showed him a neat pile of rocks.

"There's my monument," he said, "ain't that a neat piece of work? I learned how to make them from a surveyor. This tobacco can here contains my notice of location—that was a steer when I said it wasn't staked. Git down and help yourself!"

He assisted his companion, who was slightly saddle-sore, to alight and inspect the monument and then he waited expectantly.

"Oh, the mine! The mine!" cried Wunpost gaily. "Come along—have you got your sack? Well, bring along a sack and we'll fill it so full of gold it'll bust and spill out going home. Be a nice way to mark the trail, if you should want to come back sometime—and by the way, have you got that thousand dollar bill?"

"Yes, I've got it," whined the barkeeper, "but where's your cussed mine? This don't look like nothing to me!"

"No, that's it," expounded Wunpost, "you haven't got my system—they's no use for you to turn prospector. Now look in this crack—notice that stuff up and down there? Well, now, that's where I'd look to find gold."

"Jee-rusalem!" exclaimed the barkeeper, or words to that effect, and dropped down to dig out the rock. It was the very same ore that Wunpost had shown when he had entered The Mint at Blackwater, only some of it was actually richer than any of the pieces he had seen. And there was a six-inch streak of it, running down into the country-rock as if it were going to China. He dug and dug again while Wunpost, all unmindful, unpacked and cooked a good meal. Fellowes filled his small sack and all his pockets and wrapped up the rest in his handkerchief; and

121

before they packed to go he borrowed the dish-towel and went back for a last hoard of gold. It was there for the taking, and he could have all he wanted as long as he turned over the thousand dollar bill. Wunpost was insistent upon this and as they prepared to start he accepted it as payment in full.

"That's *my* idea of money!" he exclaimed admiringly as he smoothed the silken note across his knee. "A thousand dollar bill, and you could hide it inside your ear—say, wait till I pull that in Los! I'll walk up to the bar in my old, raggedy clothes and if the barkeep makes any cracks about paying in advance I'll just drop *that* down on the mahogany. That'll learn him, by grab, to keep a civil tongue in his head and to say Mister when he's speaking to a gentleman."

He grinned at the Judas that he had taken to his bosom but Fellowes did not respond. He was haunted by a fear that the simple-minded Wunpost might ask him where he got that big bill, since it is rather out of the ordinary for even a barkeeper to have that much money in his clothes; but the simple-minded Wunpost was playing a game of his own and he asked no embarrassing questions. It was taken for granted that they were both gentlemen of integrity, each playing his own system to win, and the barkeeper's nervous fear that the joker would pop up somewhere found no justification in fact.

He had his gold, all he could carry of it, and Wunpost had his thousand dollar bill, and now nothing remained to hope for but a quick trip home and a speedy deliverance from his misery.

"Say, for cripes' sake," he wailed, "ain't they any short-cut home? I'm so lame I can hardly walk."

"Well, there is," admitted Wunpost, "I could have you home by morning. But you might take to dropping that gold, like you did them Boston beans, and I'd come back to find my mine jumped."

"Oh, I won't drop no gold!" protested Fellowes earnestly, "and them beans was just for a joke. Always read about it, you know, in these here lost treasure stories; but shucks, I didn't mean no harm!"

"No," nodded Wunpost, "if I'd thought you did I'd have ditched you, back there in the rocks. But I'll tell you what I *will* do—you let me keep you blindfolded and I'll get you out of here quick."

"You're on!" agreed Fellowes and Wunpost whipped out his handkerchief and bound it across his whole face. They rode on interminably, but it was always down hill and the sagacious Mr. Fellowes even noted a deep gorge through which water was rushing in a torrent. Shortly after they passed through it he heard a rooster crow and caught the fragrance of hay and not long after that they were out on the level

123

where he could smell the rank odor of the creosote. Just at daylight they rode into Blackwater from the south, for Wunpost was still playing the game, and half an hour later every prospector was out, ostensibly hunting for his burros. But Wunpost's work was done, he turned his animals into the corral and retired for some much-needed sleep; and when he awoke the barkeeper was gone, along with everybody else in town.

The stampede was to the north and then up Jail Canyon, where there was the only hay ranch for miles; and then up the gorge and on almost to Panamint, where the tracks turned off up Woodpecker Canyon. They were back-tracking of course, for the tracks really came down it, but before the sun had set Wunpost's monument was discovered, together with the vein of gold. It was astounding, incredible, after all his early efforts, that he should let them back-track him to his mine; but that was what he had done and Pisenface Lynch was not slow to take possession of the treasure. There was no looting of the paystreak as there had been at the Willie Meena, a guard was put over it forthwith; and after he had taken a few samples from the vein Lynch returned on the gallop to Blackwater.

The great question now with Eells was how Wunpost would take it, but after hearing from his scouts that the prospector was calm he summoned him to his office. It seemed too good to be true, but so it had seemed before when Calhoun had given up the Wunpost and the Willie Meena; and when Lynch brought him in Eells was more than pleased to see that his victim was almost smiling.

"Well, followed me up again, eh?" he observed sententiously, and Eells inclined his head.

"Yes," he said, "Mr. Lynch followed your trail and—well, we have already taken possession of the mine."

"Under the contract?" inquired Wunpost and when Eells assented Wunpost shut his lips down grimly. "Good!" he said, "now I've got you where I want you. We're partners, ain't that it, under our contract? And you don't give a whoop for justice or nothing as long as you get it *all!* Well, you'll get it, Mr. Eells—do you recognize this thousand dollar bill? That was given to me by a barkeep named Fellowes, but of course he received it from you. I knowed where he got it, and I knowed what he was up to—I ain't quite as easy as I look—and now I'm going to take it and give it to a lawyer, and start in to get my rights. Yes, I've got some rights, too—never thought of that, did ye—and I'm going to demand 'em all! I'm going to go to this lawyer and put this bill in his hand and tell him to git me my *rights!* Not part of 'em, not nine tenths of 'em—I want 'em *all*—and by grab, I'm going to *get* 'em!"

He struck the mahogany table a resounding whack and Eells jumped and glanced warningly at Lynch.

"I'm going to call for a receiver, or whatever you call him, to look after my interests at the mine; and if the judge won't appoint him I'm going to have you summoned to bring the Wunpost books into court. And I'm going to prove by those books that you robbed me of my interest and never made any proper accounting; and then, by grab, he'll *have* to appoint him, and I'll get all that's coming to me, and you'll get what's coming to *you*. You'll be shown up for what you are, a low-down, sneaking thief that would steal the pennies from a blind man; you'll be showed up right, you and your sure-thing contract, and you'll get a little *publicity!* I'll just give this to the press, along with some four-bit cigars and the drinks all around for the boys, and we'll just see where you stand when you get your next rating from Bradstreet—I'll put your tin-front bank on the bum! And then I'll say to my lawyer, and he's a slippery son-of-a-goat: 'Go to it and see how much you can get—and for every dollar you collect, by hook, crook or book, I'll give you back a half of it! Sue Eells for an accounting every time he ships a brick— make him pay back what he stole on the Wunpost—give him fits over the Willie Meena—and if a half ain't enough, send him broke and you can have it *all!* Do you reckon I'll get some results?"

He asked this last softly, bowing his bristling head to where he could look Judson Eells in the eye, and the oppressor of the poor took counsel. Undoubtedly he *would* get certain results, some of which were very unpleasant to contemplate, but behind it all he felt something yet to come, some counter-proposal involving peace. For no man starts out by laying his cards on the table unless he has an ace in the hole—or unless he is running a bluff. And he knew, and Wunpost knew, that the thing which irked him most was that sure-fire Prospector's Contract. There Eells had the high card and if he played his hand well he might tame this impassioned young orator. His lawyer was not yet retained, none of the suits had been brought, and perhaps they never would be brought. Yet undoubtedly Wunpost had consulted some attorney.

"Why—yes," admitted Eells, "I'm quite sure you'd get results—but whether they would be the results you anticipate is quite another question. I have a lawyer of my own, quite a competent man and one in whom I can trust, and if it comes to a suit there's one thing you *can't* break and that is your Prospector's Contract."

He paused and over Wunpost's scowling face there flashed a twinge that betrayed him— Judson Eells had read his inner thought.

127

"Well, anyhow," he blustered, "I'll deal you so much misery—"

"Not necessary, not necessary," put in Judson Eells mildly, "I'm willing to meet you half way. What is it you want now, and if it's anything reasonable I'll be glad to consider a settlement. Litigation is expensive—it takes time and it takes money—and I'm willing to do what is right."

"Well, gimme back that contract!" blurted out Wunpost desperately, "and you can keep your doggoned mine. But if you don't by grab I'll fight you!"

"No, I can't do that," replied Eells regretfully, "and I'll tell you, Mr. Calhoun, why. You're just one of forty-odd men that have signed those Prospector's Contracts, and there's a certain principle involved. I paid out thirty thousand dollars before I got back a nickel and I can't afford to establish a precedent. If I let you buy out, they will all want to buy out—that is, if they've happened to find a mine—and the result will be that there'll be trouble and litigation every time I claim my rights. When you were wasting my grubstake I never said a word, because that, in a way, was your privilege; and now that, for some reason, you are stumbling onto mines, you ought to recognize my rights. It is a part of my policy, as laid down from the first, under no circumstances to ever release anybody;

128

otherwise some dishonest prospector might be tempted to conceal his find in the hope of getting title to it later. But now about this mine, which you have named the Stinging Lizard—what would be your top price for cash?"

"I want that contract," returned Wunpost doggedly but Judson Eells shook his head.

"How about ten thousand dollars?" suggested Eells at last, "for a quit-claim on the Stinging Lizard Mine?"

"Nothing doing!" flashed back Wunpost, "I don't sign no quit-claim—nor no other paper, for that matter. You might have it treated with invisible ink, or write something else in, up above. But—aw cripes, dang these lawyers, I don't want to monkey around—gimme a hundred thousand dollars and she's yours."

"The Stinging Lizard?" inquired Eells and wrote it absently on his blotter at which Wunpost began to sweat.

"I don't *sign* nothing!" he reminded him, and Eells smiled indulgently.

"Very well, you can acknowledge it before witnesses."

"No, I don't acknowledge nothing!" insisted Wunpost stubbornly, "and you've got to put the money in my hand. How about fifty thousand dollars and make it all cash, and I'll agree to get out of town."

"No-o, I haven't that much on hand at this

129

time," observed Judson Eells, frowning thoughtfully. "I might give you a draft on Los Angeles."

"No—cash!" challenged Wunpost, "how much have you got? Count it over and make me an offer—I want to get out of this town." He muttered uneasily and paced up and down while Judson Eells, with ponderous surety, opened up the chilled steel vault. He ran through bundles and neat packages, totting up as he went, and then with a face as frozen as a stone he came out with the currency in his hands.

"I've got twenty thousand dollars that I suppose I can spare," he began as he spread out the money, but Wunpost cut him short.

"I'll take it," he said, "and you can have the Stinging Lizard—but my word's all the quit-claim you get!"

He stuffed the money into his pockets without stopping to count it, more like a burglar than a seller of mines, and that night while the town gathered to gaze on in wonder he took the stage for Los Angeles. No one shouted good-by and he did not look back, but as they pulled out of Blackwater he smiled.

CHAPTER XII

BACK HOME

THE dry heat of July gave way to the muggy heat of August and as the September storms began to gather along the summits Wunpost Calhoun returned to his own. It was his own country, after all, this land of desert spaces and jagged mountains reared up again the sky; and he came back in style, riding a big, round-bellied mule and leading another one packed. He had a rifle under his knee, a pistol on his hip and a pair of field glasses in a case on the horn; and he rode in on a trot, looking about with a knowing smile that changed suddenly to a smirk of triumph.

"Well, well!" he exclaimed as he saw Eells emerge from the bank, "how's the mine, Mr. Eells; how's the mine?"

And Judson Eells, who had rushed out at the rumor of his approach, drew up his lip and glared at him hatefully.

"You're a criminal!" he bellowed, "I could have you jailed for this—that Stinging Lizard mine was salted!"

"The hell you say!" shrilled Wunpost and then he laughed uproariously while he did a little jig in his stirrups. "Yeee—hoo!" he yelled, "say, that's pretty good! Have you any idee who done it?"

"You did it!" answered Eells, "and I could have you arrested for it, only I don't want to have any trouble. But you agreed to leave town and now I see you're back—what's the meaning of this, Mr. Calhoun?"

"Too slow inside," complained Mr. Calhoun, who was sporting a brand-new outfit, "so I thought I'd come back and shake hands with my friends and take another look at my mine. Costs money to live in Los Angeles and I bought me a dog—looky here, cost me eight hundred dollars!"

He reached down into a nest which he had hollowed out of the pack and held up a wilted fox terrier, and as Eells stood speechless he dropped it back into its cubby-hole and laid a loving hand on the mule.

"How's this for a mule?" he enquired ingenuously, "cost me five hundred dollars in Barstow. Fastest walker in the West—picked him out on purpose—and my pack-mule can carry four hundred. How much did you lose on the Stinging Lizard?"

"I lost over thirty thousand dollars, with the road work and all," answered Eells with ponderous exactitude, and Wunpost laughed again.

"Thirty thousand!" he echoed. "I wish it was a million! But you can't say that I didn't warn you!"

132

"Warn me!" raged Eells, "you did nothing of the kind. It was a deliberate attempt to defraud me."

"Aw, cripes," scoffed Wunpost, "you can't win all the time—why don't you take your medicine like a sport? Didn't I name the danged hole the Stinging Lizard? Well, there was your warning—but you got stung!"

He laughed heartily at the joke and looked up the street, ignoring the staring crowd.

"Well, got to go!" he said. "Where *is* that road you built—like to go up and take a look at it!"

"It extends up Jail Canyon," returned the banker grimly. "I understand Mr. Campbell is using it."

"Pretty work!" exclaimed Wunpost, "won't be wasted, anyhow. That'll come in right handy for Cole. Why didn't you buy the old hassayamper out?"

"He won't sell!" grumbled Eells, "say, come in here a minute—I've got something I want to talk over."

He led the way into his inner office, where an electric fan was running, and Wunpost took off his big, black hat to loll before the breeze.

"Pretty nice," he pronounced, "they've got lots of 'em in Los. But I never suffered so much from heat in my life—the poor fools all wear *coats!* Gimme the desert, every time!"

"So you've come back to stay, eh?" inquired

Eells unsociably, "I thought you'd left these parts."

"Yep—left and came back," replied Wunpost lightly. "Say, how much do you want for that contract? You might as well release me, because it'll never buy *you* anything—you've got all the mines you'll get."

"I'll never release you!" answered Judson Eells firmly. "It's against my principles to do it."

"Aw, put a price on it," burst out Wunpost bluffly, "you know you haven't got any principles. You're out for the dough, the same as the rest of us, and you figure you'll make more by holding on. But I'm here to tell you that I'm getting too slick for you and you might as well quit while you're lucky."

"Not for any money," responded Judson Eells solemnly, "I am in this as a matter of principle."

"Ahhr, principle!" scoffed Wunpost. "You're the crookedest dog that ever drew up a contract—and then talk to me about *principle!* Why don't you say what you mean and call it your system—like they use trying to break the roulette wheel? But I'm telling you your system is played out. I'll never locate another claim as long as I live, unless I'm released from that contract; so where do you figure on any more Willie Meenas? All you'll get will be Stinging Lizards."

He burst out into taunting laughter but Judson

134

Eells sat dumb, his heavy lower lip drawn up grimly.

"That's all right," he said at last, "I have reason to believe that you have located a very rich mine—and the only way you personally can ever get a dollar out of it, is to come through and give me half!"

"The only way, eh?" jeered Wunpost, "well, where did I get the price to buy that swell pair of mules? Did I give you one-half, or even a smell? Not much—and I got this, besides."

He slapped a wad of bills that he drew from his pocket, and Eells knew they were a part of his payment—the purchase price of the salted Stinging Lizard—but he only looked them over and scowled.

"Nothing doing, eh?" observed Wunpost rising up to go, "you won't sell that contract for no price. Going to follow me up, eh, and find this hidden treasure, and skin me out of it, too? Well, hop to it, Mr. Eells, and after you've got a bellyful perhaps you'll listen to reason. You got stung good and plenty when you bought the Stinging Lizard and I figure I'm pretty well heeled. Got two new mules, beside my other animals, and an eight hundred dollar watch-dog to keep me company; and I'm going to come back inside of a month with my mules loaded down with gold. Do you reckon your pet rabbit, Mr. Phillip F. Flappum, can make me come

135

through with any part of it? Well, I consulted a lawyer before I left Los Angeles and he said—decidedly not! Your contract calls for claims, wherever located, but I haven't got any claim. This ore that I bring in may be dug from some claim, and then again it may be high-graded from some mine; but you've got to find that claim and prove that it exists before you can call for a cent. You've got to prove, by grab, where I got that gold, before you can claim that it's yours—and that's something you never can do. I'm going to say I *stole* it and if you sue for any part of it you make yourself out a thief!"

He slammed his hand on Eells' desk and slammed the door when he went out and mounted his big mule with a swagger. The citizens of Blackwater made way for him promptly, though many a lip curled in scorn, and he rode out of town sitting sideways in his saddle while he did a little jig in his stirrups. He had come into town and bearded their leading citizen and now he was on his way. If any wished to follow, that was their privilege as free citizens, and their efforts might lead them to a mine; but on the other hand they might lead them up some very rocky canyons and down through Death Valley in summer. But there was one man he knew would follow, for the stakes were high and Judson Eells was not to be denied—it was up to Lynch, who had claimed to be so bad, to prove himself a tracker and a desert-man.

Wunpost rode along slowly until the sun went down, for the heat-haze hung black over the Sink, and that evening about midnight he entered Jail Canyon on a road that was graded like a boulevard. It swung around the point well up above the creek, and then on along the wash to Corkscrew Gorge, and as he paused below the house Wunpost chuckled to himself as he thought of his boasts to Wilhelmina. He had bet her two months before that, without turning his hand over or spending a cent of money, he could build her father a road; and now here it was, laid out like a highway—a proof that his system would work. She had chosen to scoff when he had made his big talk; but here he was back with his clothes full of money, and Judson Eells had kindly built the road. He looked up at the moon, where it rose swimming through the haze, and laughed until he shook; then he camped and waited for day.

The dawn came in a wave of heat, preceding the sun like the breath from a furnace; and Wunpost woke up suddenly to hear his wilted terrier barking furiously as he raced towards the house. There was a moment of silence, then the spit and yell of a cat and as Wunpost stood grinning his dog came slinking back licking the blood from a scratch across his nose. He was a

137

full-blooded fox terrier, but small and white and trembly; and the baby-blue in his eyes pleaded of youth and inexperience as he crouched before his stern master.

"Come here!" commanded Wunpost but as he reached down to slap him a voice called his name from above.

"*Don't* whip him!" it begged and Wunpost withheld his hand for Wilhelmina had been much in his mind. She came dancing down the trail, her curls tumbling about her face and down over the perennial bib-overalls, and when the pup saw her he left his scowling master and crept meechingly to take refuge at her feet.

"He was chasing Red," she dimpled, "and you know how fierce he is—why, Red isn't afraid of a wild-cat! Where have you been? We've all been looking for you!"

"I've been in Los Angeles," responded Wunpost with a sigh, "but, by grab, I never thought that this dog of mine would get licked by an old yaller cat!"

"He isn't yellow—he's red!" corrected Wilhelmina briskly, "the desert makes all yellow cats red; but where'd you get your dog? And oh, yes; isn't it fine—how do you like our new road? They had it built up to your mine!"

"So I hear," returned Wunpost with a grim twinkle in his eye, "what do you think of my system now?"

"Why, what system?" asked Billy, staring blankly into his face, and Wunpost pulled down his lip. Was it possible that this fly-away had taken his words so lightly that she had forgotten his exposition and prophecy? Did she think that this road had come there by accident and not by deep-laid design? He called back his dog and made him lie down behind him and then he changed the subject.

"How's your father getting along?" he asked after a silence, "has he shipped out any ore? Well say, you tell 'im to get a move on. There's liable to be a cloudburst and wash the whole road out, and then where'd you be with your home stake?"

"Well, I guess there hasn't been one for over twelve years," answered Billy snapping her fingers enticingly to his dog, "and besides, it's so hot the trucks can't pull up the canyon—it makes their radiators boil. But we've got it all sacked and when Father gets his payment I'm going inside, to school. Isn't it fine, after all they said about Dad—calling him crazy and everything else—and now his mine is worth lots and lots of money! I knew all the time he would win! And Eells has been up here and offered us forty thousand dollars, but Father wouldn't even consider it."

She stepped over boldly and picked up the dog, who wriggled frantically and tried to lick her face, and Wunpost stood mumbling to himself.

So now it was her father who was getting all the credit for this wonderful stroke of luck; and he and the others who had called old Cole crazy were proven by the event to be fools. And yet he had packed ore for over two weeks to salt the Stinging Lizard for Eells!

"Put your mules in the corral and come up to breakfast!" cried Billy starting off for the house; and then she dropped his dog, which ran capering along behind her—and Wunpost had named it Good Luck! If she stole his dog on top of everything else, he would learn about women from her.

There was a cordial welcome at the house from Mrs. Campbell, who was radiant with joy over their good fortune; but Wunpost avoided the subject of the sale of his mine, for of course she must know it was salted. Anyone would know that after they had dug down a ways for Wunpost had simply quarried out a vein of rotten quartz and filled the resultant fissure with high-grade. But there is something in Latin about *caveat emptor*, which is short for "Let the buyer beware!" and if Judson Eells was so foolish as to build his road first that was certainly no fault of Wunpost's. All he had done was to locate the hole, and then Judson Eells had jumped it; and if, as a result thereof, Wunpost had trimmed him of twenty thousand, that was nothing to what Eells had done to him. And yet every time he met Mrs.

140

Campbell's eye he felt that she had her reservations about him. He was a mine-salter, a crook, the same as Eells was a crook; but she welcomed him all the same. Perhaps she held it to his credit that he had given Billy a full half when he had discovered the Willie Meena Mine; but it might be, of course, that she was this way with everyone and simply tolerated him as she did Hungry Bill. He ate a good breakfast, but without saying much, and then he went back to his camp.

Wilhelmina tagged along, joyous as a child to have company and quite innocent of what is called maidenly reserve; and Wunpost dug down into his pack and gave her a bag of candy, at the same time patting her hand.

"Yours truly," he said, "sweets to the sweet, and all that. Say, what do you think this is?"

He held up a box, which might contain almost anything that was less than six inches square, and shook his head at all her guesses.

"Come on up to the lookout," he said at last and she followed along fearlessly behind him. There are maidens, of course, who would refuse to enter dark tunnels in the company of masterful young prospectors; but Wilhelmina had yet to learn both fear and feminine subterfuge and she made no pretty excuses. She was neither afraid of the dark, nor afflicted with vertigo, nor reminded of pressing home duties;

and she was frankly interested both in the contents of the box and the ways of a man with a maid. He had given her some candy, and there was a gift in the little box—and once before he had made as if to kiss her; would he now, after bringing his lover's gifts, demand the customary tribute? And if so, should she permit it; and if not, why not?

It was very perplexing and yet Billy was determined not to evade any of the problems of life. All girls had their suitors; and yet few of them, she knew, were cast in the heroic mold of Wunpost. He was big and strong, with roving blue eyes and a smile that was both compelling and shy; and sometimes when he looked at her she felt a vague tumult, for of course he could kiss her if he would. When he had assaulted Old Whiskers and seized Dusty Rhodes by the throat, in the contest over their mine, she had stood in awe of his violence; but except for that one time when he had attempted to steal a kiss, he had reserved his rough violence for his enemies. Yet—and somehow the thought thrilled her—it might be, after all, that he was shy; and that playful, bearlike hug was only his boyish way of hinting at the wish in his heart.

It might even be that he was secretly in love with her, as she had read of other lovers in books; and that all the time, unknown to her, he was worshiping her beauty from afar. For she was

142

beautiful, she knew it—and others had told her so—and there are few girls indeed that have curling hair *and* dimples, but Nature had given her both. And now if he did not kiss her, or speak from his heart, it would be because she was dressed like a boy; and she would have to lay aside her overalls forever. For no one can hope to retain everything in this world, and life is ours to be lived; and if worst came to worst, she might give up her freedom and consent to wear millinery and skirts. She sighed and followed on, and came safely to the portal which looked out on the great world below.

Wunpost sat down deliberately at the mouth of the tunnel, on the broad seat she had built along the wall, and handed Wilhelmina the package; and as she sank down beside him the panting fox terrier slumped down at her feet and wheezed. But Billy failed to notice this sign of affection, for as the package was broken open a dainty case was exposed and this in turn revealed a pair of glasses. Not ordinary, cheap field glasses with rusty round barrels and lenses that refracted the colors of the rainbow; but exquisitely small ones, with square shoulders on the sides and quality showing in every line. She caught them up ecstatically and looked out across the Sink; and Wunpost let her gaze, though her focus was all wrong, while he made his little speech.

143

"Now," he said, "next time you see my dust you'll know whether it's a man or a dog."

"Oh, aren't they fine!" exclaimed Billy, swinging the glasses on Blackwater. "I can see every house in town. And there's a man on the trail—yes, and another one behind—I believe they're coming this way."

"Probably Pisen-face Lynch," observed Wunpost unconcernedly, "I expected him to be on my trail."

"Why, what for?" murmured Billy still struggling with the focus. "Oh, now I can see them fine! Oh, aren't these just wonderful—and such little things, too—are you going to use them to hunt horses?"

"No, they're yours!" returned Wunpost with a generous swagger, "I've got another pair of my own. I'll never forget how you picked me up that time, so this is a kind of present."

"A present!" gasped Wilhelmina and then she paused and blushed, for of course she had known it all the time. They were small glasses, for a lady, but it was nice of him to say it, and to mention her finding him on the desert. And now her mother would have to let her keep them, for they were in remembrance of her saving his life.

"It's awful kind of you," she said, "and I'll never forget it—and now, won't you show me how they work?"

She drew a little closer, and as her curls brushed his cheek Wunpost reeled as if from a blow.

"Sure," he said and gave her a kiss just as if she had really asked for it.

CHAPTER XIII

WITH HAY HOOKS

IT is no more than right that the first kiss should be forgiven, especially if no one is to blame, and Wilhelmina forgave him very sweetly; but there was a wild, hunted look in Wunpost's bold eyes and he wondered what would happen next. Something had come over him very suddenly and made him forget the restraint which all ladies, even in overalls, laid upon him; and when their hands had touched some great force had drawn them together and he had kissed her before she knew it. But instead of resisting she had yielded for a moment, and then pushed him away very slowly; and he still remembered, like part of a dream, her heart beating against his breast. But it was all over now, and she was toying with the field glasses which he had brought from the city as a present.

"Isn't it wonderful," she said, "how we first came together? And the first place I looked for when you gave me these glasses was that wash where you made your two fires."

"If you'd had them then," ventured Wunpost at last, "you'd 've been able to see me plain."

"Yes," she sighed, "but I found you anyhow.

146

Doesn't it seem a long time ago? And it was only the end of last May."

"Something doing every minute," burst out Wunpost gaily, "say, I've found two mines this summer! What did old Eells think of the Stinging Lizard? I hooked him right on that—he'll be careful what he grabs next time. And when he jumps the next claim of mine I reckon he'll sink a few feet before he builds any more ten thousand dollar roads!"

He chuckled and ran his hand through his tumbled hair, which always stood straight on end, but Billy was looking at him curiously.

"Mr. Eells was up to see us," she said at last, "and he claims you salted that mine. And he even told Father that you located it up our canyon just on purpose so we could use his road!"

"And what did you say?" inquired Wunpost teasingly. "Didn't I tell you, right here, I was going to do it?"

"Oh, but you were just fooling!" she protested laughing, "and I told him you did nothing of the kind. And then Father stepped in, when he heard what we were talking about, and he told Mr. Eells what he thought of him."

"No, but I did salt the mine!" spoke up Wunpost quickly, "there wasn't any fooling there. And, being as I had to locate it somewhere—well, the chances are Eells was correct."

147

"Oh, that's just the way you talk!" she burst out incredulously, "did you honestly do it on purpose?"

"Well, I guess I did!" boasted Wunpost. "I just stopped over in Blackwater and told Mr. Eells about it. So don't be worried on my account— and he built you a mighty good road."

"Yes, but do you think it was quite right," began Billy indignantly, "to make Father seem a party to a fraud? It's what some people would call a very shady transaction; but I suppose, of course, you're proud of it!"

"Why, sure I am!" returned Wunpost warmly, "and you don't need to be so high and mighty. I guess I'm just as good as your old man or anybody, and I notice he's using the road!"

"He won't though," answered Billy, "if I tell him what's happened! My father is honest, he works for what he gets, and that road is just the same as stolen!"

"Well, go ahead and tell him!" challenged Wunpost angrily. "We'll come to a show-down, right now. And anybody that's too good to use my road is too good to associate with *me!*" He brought down his big fist into the palm of his hand and Wilhelmina jumped at the smack. "Didn't I tell you," he demanded rising and pointing at her accusingly, "didn't I say I was going to build that road? Well, why didn't you kick about it *then?* You were game to follow me

148

up and jump my mine so your father could build him a road; but the minute I trim old Eells, who has robbed you of a million, by grab, all of a sudden you get *good!* You can't bear to use a road that that old skinflint built, thinking he'd robbed me of another rich mine! No, that wouldn't be right, that's a shady transaction! All right then, don't use the doggoned road!"

He smashed his fist into his hand in a final sweeping gesture of disdain and Wilhelmina gazed at him fixedly.

"I thought you were just talking," she said at last, "but don't you ever tell Father what's happened. If you do he'll never use the road—or if he does, he'll pay Mr. Eells for it. He tries to be honest in everything."

"Yes, and look what it gets him!" cried Wunpost passionately, "he's spent half his life in this hell-hole of a canyon and you're chasing around here in overalls! And then when some *crook* like me comes along and gives him a ten thousand dollar road this is all the thanks he gets! I'm through—you can rustle for yourself!"

"Very well!" returned Billy with a wild gleam in her eye, "and if you don't like my overalls—"

"I do!" he broke in, "I like 'em fine—like 'em better than those flimsy danged skirts! But if you're too good to use my road—"

"It isn't that," interrupted Billy, "I'm glad you built the road, but Father looks at it differently.

149

He told Mr. Eells he wouldn't be a party to any such scheme to defraud. But—now it's all built—don't tell him how you did it; because I want him to have a little happiness. He's been working so long and this came, as he said, just like an act of Providence; so let's not tell him, and when he's taken out his ore he can pay Mr. Eells, if he wishes to."

"If he's crazy!" corrected Wunpost. "What, pay that crook? Say, do you see those two men on the trail? They're hired by Eells to tag along behind me and trail me to my mine. Now what right has he got to claim that mine? Did he ever give me a dollar to spend, while I was up there in the high country looking for it? He did not, and he stole every dollar I had before I ever went out to prospect. Didn't he rob us both of the Willie Meena—take it all without giving us a cent? Well, what's the sense of trying to treat him white, when you know he's out to do you? His name is Eells and he skins 'em alive! But you wait—I'm out to skin *him!*"

"You're awfully convincing," conceded Billy smiling tremulously, "but somehow it doesn't seem right. Just because he robs you—"

"Aw, forget it; forget it!" exclaimed Wunpost impatiently, "didn't I tell you this is no Sunday school picnic? What're you going to do, let him go on robbing everybody until he has all the money in the world? No, you've got to play the

150

game—go after him with the hay hooks and get his back hair if you can! I've trimmed him of twenty thousand and a ten thousand dollar road, but where did he get all that coin? He took it out of our mine, the old Willie Meena, and a whole lot more besides. Well, whose money was it, anyway—didn't I own the mine first? All right, then, I reckon it was *mine!*"

He patted his pocket, where his roll of bills lay, and smiled roguishly as he grabbed up the dog.

"Fine pup, eh?" he began, "well, he picked me out himself—followed along when I was going down the street. Tried to lose him and couldn't do it, he followed me everywhere, so I kept him and called him Good Luck. Get the idea? Luck is my pup, he lays down and rolls over whenever I say the word. Going to make a fine watchdog if he lives through this hot weather—how'd you like to keep him a while?"

"Oh, I'd like to!" beamed Billy, "only I'm afraid you might be jealous—"

"Not of no pup, kid," returned Wunpost with his lordliest swagger, "and if you steal him, by grab you can have him!"

"Well, I'll bet I can do it!" answered Billy defiantly. "And are you still going to give me that mine?"

"If you can find it!" nodded Wunpost. "Or I'll give it to Mr. Lynch, if he'll promise to follow the leader. I see that's an Injun that he's got riding along behind him but I'm going to lose 'em both. These Shooshonnies ain't so much—I can out-trail 'em, any time—and I tell you what I'm going to do. I'm going to lead Mr. Lynch and his rat-eating guide just as long as they're game to follow, and if they follow me two weeks I'll take 'em to my mine and tell 'em to help themselves. Now that's sporting, ain't it? Because the Sockdolager ain't staked and she's the richest hole I've struck."

"Yes, it's sporting," she admitted, "but why don't you stake it? Are you afraid they'll take it away from you?"

"Don't you think it!" he exclaimed, "if it was staked I'd have half of it! No, I'm doing this out of pride. I'm leaving that claim open and if Mr. Eells can find it he's welcome to it *all!* But I'm telling you, it'll never be found!"

He nodded impressively, with a wise, mysterious smile, and Billy rose up impatiently.

"I believe you *like* to fight," she stated accusingly and Wunpost did not deny it.

CHAPTER XIV

POISONED BAIT

THE fight for the Sockdolager Mine was on and Wunpost led off up the canyon with a swagger. His fast walking mule stepped off at a brisk pace and the pack-mule, well loaded with provisions and grain, followed along up Judson Eell's road. First it led through the Gorge, now clinging to one wall and now crossing perforce to the other, and as Wunpost saw the work of the powder-men above him he laughed and slapped his leg. Great masses of rock had been shot down from the sides, filling up the pot-holes which the cloudburst had dug; and then, along the sides, a grade had been constructed which gave clearance for loaded trucks. Past the Gorge, the work showed the signs of greater haste, as if Eells had driven his men to the limit; but to get through at all he had had to move much dirt, and that of course had run into money. Wunpost ambled along luxuriously, chuckling at each heavy job of blasting and at the spot where Cole Campbell's road turned in; and then he swung off up Woodpecker Canyon to where the Stinging Lizard Mine had been located.

Great timbers still lay where they had been

dumped from the trucks, there was a concrete foundation for the engine; and a double-compartment shaft, sunk on the salted vein, showed what great expectations had been blasted. With the Willie Meena still sinking on high-grade ore, Judson Eells had taken a good deal for granted when he had set out to develop the Stinging Lizard. He had squared out his shaft and sunk on the vein only as far as the muckers could throw out the waste; and then, instead of installing a windlass or a whim, he had decided upon a gallows-frame and hoist. But to bring in his machinery he must first have a road, for the trail was all but impassable; and so, without sinking, he had blasted his way up the canyon, only to find his efforts wasted. The ore had been dug out before his engine was installed, thus saving him even greater loss; but every dollar that he had put into the work had been absolutely thrown away. Wunpost camped there and gloated and then, shortly after midnight, he set off with his tongue in his cheek.

The time had now come when he was to match wits with Lynch in the old game of follow-my-leader and, even with the Indian to do Lynch's tracking, he had no fears for the outcome. There were places on those peaks where a man could travel for miles without placing his foot on soft ground, and other places in Death Valley where he could travel in sand that was so powdery it

154

would bog a butterfly. First the high places, to wear them out and make Pisen-face Lynch get quarrelsome; and then the desolate Valley, with its heat and poison springs, to put the final touch to his revenge. For it was revenge that Wunpost sought, revenge on Pisen-face Lynch, who had driven him from two claims with a gun; and this chase over the hills, which had started so casually, had really been planned for months. It was part of that "system" which he had developed so belatedly, by which his enemies were all to be confounded; and, knowing that Lynch would follow wherever he led, Wunpost had made his plans accordingly. He was leading the way into a trap, long set, which was sure to enmesh its prey.

At daylight Wunpost paused in his steady, plunging climb and looked back over the rock-slides and boulders; and while his mules munched their grain well back out of sight he focused his new field glasses and watched. From the knife-blade ridge up which he had spurred and scrambled the whole country lay before him like a relief map, and in the particular gash-like canyon where he had located the Stinging Lizard he made out his furtive pursuers. The Indian was ahead, leaning over in his saddle as he kept his eyes on the trail; and Lynch rode behind, a heavy rifle beneath his knee, scanning the ridges to prevent a surprise. But neither led a pack-horse and when Wunpost had looked his fill he put up his glasses and smiled.

In the country where he was going there was no grass for those horses, no browse that even an Indian pony could travel on; and if they wanted to keep up with him and his grain-fed mules they would have to use quirt and spurs. And the man who feeds his horse on buckskin alone is due to walk back to camp. So reasoned John C. Calhoun from his cow-puncher days, when he had tried out the weaknesses of horseflesh; and as he returned to the grassy swale where his mules were hid he looked them over proudly. His riding mule, Old Walker, was still in his prime, a big-bellied animal with the long reach in its fore-shoulders which made it by nature a fast walker; and his pack-mule, equally round-bellied to store away food, was short-bodied as well so that he bore his pack easily without any tendency to give down. He had been raised with Old Walker and would follow him anywhere, without being dragged by a rope, so that Wunpost had both hands for any emergency which might arise and could keep his eyes on the trail.

And to think that these noble animals, big and black and beautifully gaited, had been bought with Judson Eells' own money; while he, poor fool, sent Lynch out after him on a miserable Indian cayuse. Wunpost's road was always plain, for where he went they must follow, but at every rocky point or granite-strewn flat they must circle and cut for his trail. As he rode on now to the north he did not double and twist, for the Indian would know the old trail; but the tracks he had left behind him before he mounted to the ridge were as aimless as it was possible to make them. They did not strike out boldly up some hogback or canyon but at every fork and bend they turned this way and that, as if he were hopelessly lost. And now as he rode on, unobserved by his pursuers, over the wellworn Indian trail along the summit, Lynch and his tracker were far behind, tracing his mule-tracks to and fro, up and down the broiling hot canyons.

On the summit it was cool and the grass was still green, for the snow had held late on the peaks, and the junipers and piñons had given place to oaks and limber pines which stood up along the steep slopes like switches. The air was sweet and pure, all the world lay below him; but, as the heat came on, the abyss of Death Valley was lost in a pall of black haze. It gathered from nowhere, smoke-like and yet not smoke; a haze, a murk, a mass of writhing heat like the fumes from a witches' cauldron. Wunpost had simmered in that cauldron, and he would simmer again soon; but gladly, if he had Lynch for company. It was follow-my-leader and, since there were no long wharves to jump off of, Wunpost had decided upon the Valley of Death.

And if, in following after him to rob him of his mine, Pisen-face Lynch should succumb to the heat, that might justly be considered a visitation of Providence to punish him for his misspent life. Or at least so Wunpost reasoned and, remembering the gun under Lynch's knee, he decided to keep well in the lead.

Wunpost camped that night at the upper water in Wild Rose Canyon, letting his mules get a last feed of grass; and the next morning at daylight he was up and away on the long trail that led down to Death Valley. But first it led north over a broad, sandy plain, where Indian ponies were grazing in stray bands; and then, after ten miles, it swung off to the east where it broke through the hills and turned down. After that it was a jump-off for six thousand feet, from the mountain-top to down below sea-level; and, before he lost himself in the gap between the hills, Wunpost paused and looked back across the plain.

This was the door to his trap, for at the edge of the rim the trail split in twain; the Wet Trail leading past water while the Dry Trail was shorter, but dry. And as live bait is best he unpacked and waited patiently until he spied his pursuers in the pass. They were not five miles away, coming down the narrow draw which marked the turn in the trail, and after a long look Wunpost put up his glasses and saddled and packed to go. Yet still he lingered on, looking back through the shimmering heat that seemed to make the yellow earth blaze; until at last they were so near that he could see them point ahead and bring their tired horses to a stop. Then he whipped out his pistol and shot back at them defiantly, turning off up the Dry Trail at a trot.

They followed, but cautiously, as if anxious to avoid a conflict and Wunpost swung off between the points of two hills and led them on down the dry canyon. If they took the Wet Trail, which the Indian knew, he might double back and give them the slip; but now there was no water till they had descended to sea-level and crossed the treacherous corduroy to Furnace Creek. The trap was sprung, they were committed to the adventure, to follow him wherever he might lead; and Wunpost never stopped spurring until he had descended the steep canyon and led them out in the dry wash below. It was like climbing down a wall into a sink-hole of boiling heat, but Lynch did not weaken and Wunpost bowed his head and took the main trail to the ranch.

The sun swung low behind the rim of the Panamints, throwing a shadow across the broad canyon below; ten miles to the east, under the heat and haze, lay Furnace Creek Ranch and rest; but as his pursuers came on, just keeping within sight of him, Wunpost turned off sharply to the north. He quit the trail and struck out across the boulder-patches towards the point of Tucki Mountain, and if they followed him there it would be into a country that even the Indians were afraid of. It was there that Death Valley had earned its name, when a party of Mormon emigrants had died beside their ox-teams after drinking the water at Salt Creek. There was Stove-pipe Hole, with the grave close by of the man who had not stopped to bail the hole; and, nearest of all, was Poison Spring, the worst water in all Death Valley. Wunpost turned out and started north, daring his enemies to follow, and Lynch accepted the challenge—alone.

The Indian rode on, leaving the white man to his fate and heading for Furnace Creek Ranch; and Wunpost, sweating streams and cursing to himself, flogged on toward Poison Spring. It was a hideous thing to do, but Lynch had chosen to follow him and his blood would be upon his own head. Wunpost had given him the trail, to go on to the ranch while he turned back the way they had come; but no, Lynch was bull-headed, or perhaps the heat had warped his judgment—in any case he had elected to follow. The last courtesies were past, Wunpost had given him his chance, and Lynch had taken his trail like a bloodhound; he could not claim now that he was going in the same direction—he was following along after him like a murderer. Perhaps the slow fever of the terrible heat had turned his anger

160

into an obsession to kill, for Wunpost himself was beginning to feel the desert madness and he set out deliberately to lure him.

Where the black and frowning ramparts of Tucki Mountain thrust out towards the edge of the Sink a spring of stinking water rises up from the ground and runs off into the marsh. From the peaks above, it is a bright strip of green at which the wary mountain sheep gaze longingly; but down in that rank grass there are bones and curling horns that have taught the survivors to beware. It is Poison Spring, *the* Poison Spring in a land where all water is bad; and in many a long day Wunpost was the only human being who had gazed into its crystal depths. For the water was clear, too clear to be good, without even a green scum along its edge; and the rank, deceiving grass which grew up below could not tempt him to more than taste it. But, being trailed at the time by some men from Nevada who had seen the Sockdolager ore, he had conceived a possible use for the spring; and, coming back later, he had buried two cans of good water where he could find them when occasion demanded. This was the trap, in fact, toward which for four days he had been leading his vindictive pursuers; it was poisoned bait, laid out by Nature herself, to strike down such coyotes as Lynch.

Wunpost arrived at Poison Spring well along in the evening, the desert night being almost turned to day by the splendor of a waning moon. He rode in across the flat and down the salt-encrusted bank, still sweltering in the smothering heat; and the pounding blood in his brain had brought on a kind of fury—a death-anger at Pisen-face Lynch. He dug into the sand and drew out the cans of water, holding his mules away from the spring; and then, from a bucket, he gave each a small drink after taking a large one himself. There were two five-gallon cans, and after he had finished he lashed the full one on the pack; the other one, which sloshed faintly if one shook it up and down, he tossed mockingly down by the spring. And then he rode on, wiping the sweat from his brow and gazing back grimly into the night.

CHAPTER XV

WUNPOST TAKES THEM ALL ON

THE morning found Wunpost at Salt Creek Crossing, where the bones of a hundred emigrants lie buried in the sand without even a cross to mark their resting place. It was a place well calculated to bring up thoughts of death, but Wunpost faced the coming day calmly. At the first flush of dawn the sand was still hot from the sun of the evening before; the low air seemed to suffocate him with its below-sea-level pressure, and the salt marshes to give off stinking gases; it was a hell-hole, even then, and the day was yet to come, when the Valley would make life a torment.

The white borax-flats would reflect a blinding light, the briny marshes would seethe in the sun; and every rock, every sand-dune, would radiate more heat to add to the flame in the sky. Wunpost knew it well, the long-enduring agony which would be his lot that day; but he moved about briskly, bailing the slime from the well and sinking it deeper into the sand. He doused his body into the water and let his pores drink, and threw buckets of it on his beseeching mules; but only after the well-hole had been scraped and bailed twice would he permit them to drink the brackish water. Then he tied them in the shade of the wilting mesquite trees and strode to the top of the hill.

A man, perforce, takes on the color of his surroundings, and Wunpost was coated white from the crystallized salt and baked black underneath by the glare; but the look in his eyes was as savage and implacable as that of a devil from hell. He sat down on the point and focussed his glasses on Poison Spring, and then on the trail beyond; and at last, out on the marshes, he saw an object that moved—it was Pisen-face Lynch and his horse. The horse was in the lead, picking his way along a trail which led across the Sink towards the Ranch; and Lynch was behind, following feebly and sinking down, then springing up again and struggling on. His way led over hummocks of solid salt, across mud-holes and borax-encrusted flats; and far to the south another form moved towards him—it was the Indian, riding out to bring him in.

The sun swung up high, striking through Wunpost's thin shirt like the blast from a furnace door; sweat rolled down his face, to be sopped up by the bath-towel which he wore draped about his neck; but he sat on his hilltop, grim as a gargoyle on Notre Dame, gloating down on the suffering man. This was Pisen-face Lynch, the bad man from Bodie, who was going to trail him to his mine; this was Eells' hired man-killer and professional claim-jumper who had robbed him of the Wunpost and Willie Meena—and now he was a derelict, lost on the desert he claimed to know, following along behind his half-dead horse; and but for the Indian who was coming out to meet him he would go to his just reward. Wunpost put up his glasses and turned back with a grin—it was hell, but he was getting his revenge.

Wunpost spent the heat of the day in the bottom of the well, floating about like a frog in the brine, but as evening came on he crawled out dripping and saddled up and packed in haste. Every cinch-ring was searing hot, even the wood and leather burned him, and as he threw on the packs he lifted one foot after the other in a devil's dance over the hot sands. It was hot even for Death Valley, the hottest place in North America, but there was no use in waiting for it to cool. Wunpost soused himself and mounted, and the next morning at dawn he looked down from the rim of the Panamints.

The great sink-hole was beginning to seethe, to give off its poisonous vapors and fill up like a bowl with its own heat; but he had escaped it and fled to the heights while Pisen-face Lynch stayed below. He was still at the ranch, gasping for breath before the water-fan which served to keep the men there alive; and as he breathed that bone-dry air and felt the day's heat coming on, he was cursing the name of Calhoun. Yes, cursing long and loud, or deep and low, and vowing to wreak his revenge; for before he had worked for hire, but now he had a grievance of his own. He would take up Wunpost's trail like an Indian on the warpath, like a warrior who had been robbed of his medicine-bag; he would come on the run and with blood in his eye—that is, if the heat had not killed him. For his pride was involved, and his name as a trailer and an all-around desert-man; he had been led into a trap by a boy in his twenties, and it was up to him to demonstrate or quit.

Wunpost went his way tranquilly, for there was no one to pursue him; and ten days later he rode down Jail Canyon with his pack-mule loaded with ore. It had been his boast that he would return in two weeks with a mule-load of Sockdolager gold; but Billy, as usual, had taken his boast lightly and came running with news of her own.

"Hello!" she called. "Say, you can't guess what I've done—I've taught Red and Good Luck to be friends. They eat their supper together!"

"Good!" observed Wunpost, "and not to change the subject, what's the chances for a white man to eat? I've been living on jerky for three days."

"Why, they're good," returned Billy, suddenly

166

quieted by his manner. "What's the matter—have you had any trouble?"

"Oh, no!" blustered Wunpost, "nah, nothing like that—the other fellow had all the trouble. Did Pisen-face Lynch and that Injun come back? Well, I'll bet they were dragging their tracks out!"

"They didn't come through here, but I saw them on the trail—it must have been a week ago. But what's all that that you've got in your pack-sacks—have you been out and got some more ore?"

"Why, sure," answered Wunpost, deftly easing off his kyacks and lowering the load to the ground. "Didn't I tell you I was going to get some?"

"Yes, but—"

"But what?" he demanded, looking down on her arrogantly, and Wilhelmina became interested in the dog.

"You have such a funny way of talking," she said at last, "and besides—would you mind letting me look at it?"

"I sure would!" replied Wunpost; "you leave them sacks alone. And any time my word ain't as good as gold—"

"Oh, of course it's good!" she protested, and he took her at her word.

"All right, then—I've got the gold."

"Oh, have you really?" she cried, and as he

167

rolled his eyes accusingly she laughed and bit her lip. "That's just *my* way of talking," she explained, rather lamely. "I mean I'm glad—and surprised."

"Well, you'll be more surprised," he said, nodding grimly, "when I show you a piece of the ore. I sold that last lot to a jeweler in Los Angeles for twenty-four dollars an ounce, quartz and all—and pure gold is worth a little over twenty. Talk about your jewelry ore! Wait till I show this in Blackwater and watch them saloon-bums come through here. Too lazy to go out and find anything for themselves—all they know is to follow some poor guy like me and rob him of what he finds. What's the news from down below?"

"Oh, nothing," answered Billy, and stood watching him doubtfully as he unsaddled and turned out his gaunted mules. His new black hat was sweated through already and his clothes were salt-stained and worn, but it was the look in his eye even more than his clothes which convinced her he had had a hard trip. He was close-mouthed and grim and the old rollicking smile seemed to have been lost beneath a two weeks' growth of beard. Perhaps she had done wrong to speak of the dog first, but she knew there was something behind.

"Did you have a fight with Mr. Lynch?" she asked at last, and he darted a quick glance and said nothing. "Because when he went through here," she went on finally, "he seemed to be awful quarrelsome."

"Yes, he's quarrelsome," admitted Wunpost, "but so am I. You wait till I tangle with him, sometime."

"You're hungry!" she declared, still gazing at him fixedly, and he gave way to a twisted grin.

"How'd you guess it?" he inquired; but she did not tell him, for of course they were supposed to be friends. Yes, good friends, and more—she had let him kiss her once, but now he seemed to have forgotten it. He ate supper greedily and went back to the corral to sleep, and in the morning he was gone.

The early-risers at Blackwater, out to look for their burros or to get a little eye-opener at the saloon, were astonished to see his mules in the adobe corral and Wunpost himself on the street. He was reputed to be in hiding from Pisen-face Lynch, who had been inquiring for him for over a week; and the news was soon passed to Lynch himself, for Blackwater had a grudge against Wunpost. He had made the town, yes, in a manner of speaking—for of course he had discovered the Willie Meena Mine and brought in Eells and the boomers—but never to their knowledge had he spoken a good word of them, or of anything else in town. He came swaggering down their streets as if he owned the place, or

169

had enough money to buy it—and besides, he had led them on two disastrous stampedes in which no one had even located a claim. And the Stinging Lizard Mine was salted! Hence their haste to tell Lynch and the malevolent zeal with which they maneuvered to bring them together.

Wunpost was standing before the Express office, waiting for the agent to open up and receive his ore-sacks for shipment, when he espied his enemy advancing, closely followed by an expectant crowd. Lynch was still haggard and emaciated from his hard trip through Death Valley, and his face had the pallor of indoors; but his small, hateful eyes seemed to burn in their sockets and he walked with venomous quickness. But Wunpost stood waiting, his head thrust out and his gun pulled well to the front, and Lynch came to a sudden halt.

"So there you are!" he burst out accusingly, "you low-down, poisoning whelp! You poisoned that water, you know you did, and I've a danged good mind to kill ye!"

"Hop to it!" invited Wunpost, "just git them rubbernecks away. I ain't scared of you or nobody!"

He paused, and the rubbernecks betook themselves away, but Pisen-face Lynch did not shoot. He stood in the street, shifting his feet uneasily, and Wunpost opened the vials of scorn.

"You're bad, ain't you?" he taunted. "You're so

bad your face hurts you, but you can't run no blazer on me. And just because you chased me clean down into Death Valley you don't need to think I'm afraid. I was just showing you up as a desert-man, et cetery, but if any man had told me you'd drink that poisoned water I'd 've said he was crazy with the heat. You're a lovely looking specimen of humanity! What's the matter—didn't you like them Epsom salts?"

"There was arsenic in that water!" charged Pisen-face fiercely. "I had it analyzed—you were trying to kill me!"

"Why, sure there was arsenic," returned Wunpost mockingly, "don't you know that rank, fishy smell? But don't blame me—it was God Almighty that threw the mixture together. And didn't I leave you a drink in that empty can? Well, where is your proper gratitude?"

He ogled him sarcastically and Lynch took a step forward, only to halt as Wunpost stepped to meet him.

"That's all right!" threatened Lynch, his voice tremulous with rage and weakness. "You wait till I git back my strength. I'll fix you for this, you dirty, poisoning coward—you led me to that spring on purpose!"

"Yes, and you followed, you sucker!" returned Wunpost insultingly; "even your Injun had better sense than that. What did you expect me to do—leave you a canteen of good water so you could trail me up and pot me? No, you can consider yourself lucky I didn't shoot you like a dog for following me off the trail. I gave you the road—what did you want to follow *me* for? By grab, it looked danged bad!"

"I'll go where I please!" declared Lynch defiantly. "You're hiding a mine that belongs to Mr. Eells and my instructions were to follow you and find it."

"Well, if you'd followed your instructions," returned Wunpost easily, "you sure would have found a mine. Do you see these two bags? Plum full of ore that I dug since I gave you the shake. Go back and report that to your boss."

"You're a liar!" snarled Lynch, but his eyes were on the ore-sacks and now they were gleaming with envy. And other eyes also were suddenly focused on the gold, at which Wunpost surveyed the crowd intolerantly.

"You're a prize bunch of prospectors," he announced as from the housetops. "Why don't you get out in the hills and rustle? That's the way I got my start. But you Blackwater stiffs want to hang around town and let somebody else do the work. All you want is a chance to stake an extension on some big strike, so you can sell it to some promoter from Los!"

He grunted contemptuously and picked up the two big sacks while the citizens of Blackwater sneered back at him.

"Aw, bull!" scoffed one, "you ain't got no gold! And if you have, by grab, you stole it. What about the Stinging Lizard?"

"Well, *what* about it?" retorted Wunpost, giving his bags to the Express agent, "—put down the value on that at seven thousand dollars." This last was aside to the inquiring Express agent, but the crowd heard it and burst out hooting.

"Seven thousands *cents!*" yelled a voice; "you never *saw* seven thousand dollars! You're a bull-shover and your mine was salted!"

"Sure it was salted!" agreed Wunpost, laughing exultantly, "but you Blackwater stiffs will bite at anything. Did *I* ever claim it was a mine? I'm a bull-shover, am I? Well, when did I ever come here and try to sell somebody a mine? No; I came into town with some Sockdolager ore, and you dastards all tried to get me drunk; and I finally made a deal with the barkeep at The Mint to show him the place for a thousand dollar bill. Well, didn't I show him the place—and didn't he come back more than satisfied with his pockets bursting out with the gold? *He* never had no kick—I met him in Los Angeles and he told me he had sold the rock for thirteen hundred dollars to a jeweler. But say, my friends, don't you think I knew where he would go to get that thousand dollar bill? Do you think I was so drunk I expected a barkeeper to have thousand dollar

173

bills in his pocket? No; I knowed who he would go to, and Eells gave him the bill and a pocket full of Boston beans; but he lost them on the road, so I brought him down Jail Canyon and old-scout Lynch here, he followed my tracks!

"Wasn't that wonderful, now? He followed our tracks back and he found the Stinging Lizard Mine—and then, of course, he jumped it! That's his job, when he ain't licking old Judson Eells' boots or framing up some crooked deal with Flappum; and then he went back and told Eells. And then Eells—you know him—being as he'd stole the mine from me, like all crooks he thought it was valuable. Was it up to me then to go to Mr. Eells and tell him that the mine was salted? Would *you* have done it—would *anybody?* Well, he thought he had me cinched, and I sold out for twenty thousand dollars. And now, my friend, you said a moment ago that I'd never *seen* seven thousand dollars. All right, I say *you* never did! But just, by grab, to show you who's four-flushing I'll put you out of your misery—I'll *show* you seven thousand, savvy?"

He stuck out his head and gazed insolently into the man's face and then drew out his wad of bills. They were badly sweated, but the numbers were there—he peeled off seven bills and waved them airily, then laughed and shoved them into his overalls.

"Tuh hell with you!" he burst out defiantly,

174

consigning all Blackwater to perdition with one grand, oratorical flourish. "You think you're so smart," he went on tauntingly, "now come and trail me to my mine. If you find it you can have it—it ain't even staked—but they ain't one of you dares to follow me. I ain't afraid of Eells and his hired yaller dog, and I ain't afraid of *you!* I'll take you *all* on—old Eells and all the rest of you—and I ain't afraid to show you the ore!"

He strode into the Express office and grabbed up a sack, which he cut open with a slash of his knife; and then he reached in and took out a great chunk that bulged and gleamed with gold.

"Am I four-flushing?" he inquired, and when no one answered he grunted and tied up the hole. There was a silence, and the crowd began to filter away—all but Lynch, who stood staring like an Indian. Then he too turned away, his haggard eyes blinking fast, like a woman on the verge of bitter tears.

CHAPTER XVI

DIVINE PROVIDENCE

THE thundercaps were gleaming like silver in the heat when Wunpost rode back to Jail Canyon; but he came on almost merrily, a sopping bath-towel about his neck and his shirt pulled out, like a Chinaman's. These were the last days of September, when the clouds which had gathered for months at last were giving down their rain; and the air, now it was humid, seemed to open every pore and make the sweat run in rivulets. Wunpost perspired, but he was happy, and as he neared the silent house he whistled shrilly for his dog. Good Luck came out for a moment, looked down at him reproachfully, and crawled back under the house. Yes, it was hot in the canyon, for the ridge cut off the wind and the rimrock reflected yet more heat, but Wunpost was happy through it all. He had told Blackwater where it could go.

Not Eells and Lynch alone, but the citizens at large, collectively and as individuals; and he had planted the seeds of envy and rage to rankle in their hairy breasts. He had shown them his gold, to make them yearn to find it, and his money to make them envy him his wealth; and then he had left them to stew in their own juice, for

Blackwater was as hot as Jail Canyon. He was riding a horse now, and, in addition to Old Walker, he had a third mule, heavily packed; and he was headed for the hills to hide still more food and water against the chase that was sure to come. Sooner or later they would follow on his trail, those petty, hateful souls who now sat in the barrooms and gasped like fish for breath; but they were waiting, forsooth, for the weather to cool down and the cloudbursts to finish their destruction. And that was the very reason why they would never find his mine—they were afraid to take his chances.

Mrs. Campbell and Wilhelmina were out on the back porch, which had been sprinkled until it was almost cool; and when Wunpost had unpacked and put his mules in the corral he came up the hill and joined them. Wilhelmina had returned to her proper sphere, being clothed in the filmiest of gowns; and poor Mrs. Campbell, who was nearly prostrated by the heat, allowed her to entertain the company. They sat in the dense shade of the umbrella trees and creepers, within easy reach of a dripping olla; and after taking a huge drink, which started the sweat again, Wunpost sank down on the cool dirt floor.

"It ain't so hot here!" he began encouragingly; "you ought to be down in Blackwater. Say, the wind off that Sink would make your hair curl. I scared a lizard out of the shade and he hadn't run

177

ten feet till he disappeared in a puff of smoke. His pardner turned over and started to lick his toes—"

"Yes, it does look like rain," observed Billy with a twinkle. "How long since *you* started to herd lizards?"

"Who—me?" inquired Wunpost. "W'y, I'm telling you the truth. But say, it does look like rain. If they'd only spread it out, instead of dumping it all in one place, it'd suit me better, personally. There was a cloudburst last week hit into the canyon above me and I just made my getaway in time, and where that water landed you'd think a hydraulic sluice had been washing down the hill for a year. It all struck in one place and gouged clean down to bedrock, and when she came by me there was so much brush pushed ahead that it looked like a big, moving dam. Where's your father—up getting out ore?"

"Yes, he's up at the mine," spoke up Mrs. Campbell, "although I've begged him not to work so hard. The heat is almost killing him, but he's so thankful to have his road done that he won't delay a minute. He's used up all his sacks, but he's still sorting the ore so that he can load it right onto the trucks."

"Yes, that's good," commented Wunpost, glancing furtively at Billy, "I hope he makes a million. He deserves it—he's sure worked hard."

"Yes, he has," responded Mrs. Campbell, "and

I've always had faith in him, but others have tried to discourage him. I believe I've heard you say that his work was all wasted, but now everybody is envying him his success. It all goes to show that the Lord cares for his own, and that the righteous are not forgotten; because Cole has always said he would rather be poor and honest than to own the greatest fortune in the land. And now it seems as if the hand of Providence has just reached down and given us our road—the Lord provides for his own."

"Looks that way," agreed Wunpost; "sure treating *me* fine, too. There was a time, back there, when He seemed to have a copper on every bet I played, but now luck is coming my way. Of course I don't deserve it—and for that matter, I don't ask no odds—but this last mine I found is a Sockdolager right, and Eells or none of 'em can't find it. I took down one mule-load that was worth ten thousand dollars, and when I was shipping it you should have seen them Blackwater bums looking on with tears in their eyes. That's all right about the Lord providing for his own, but I tell you hard work has got something to do with it, whether you believe in religion or not. I'm a rustler, I'll say that, and I work for what I get, just as hard as your husband or anyone—"

"Ah, but Mister Calhoun," broke in Mrs. Campbell reproachfully, "we've heard evil

179

stories of your dealings with Eells. Not that we like him, for we don't; but, so we are informed, the mine that you sold him was salted."

"Why, mother!" exclaimed Billy, but the fat was in the fire, for Wunpost had nodded shamelessly.

"Yes," he said, "the mine was salted, but don't let that keep you awake nights. I didn't *sell* him the mine—he took it away from me and gave me twenty thousand for a quit-claim. And the twenty thousand dollars was nothing to what I lost when he robbed me and Billy of our mine."

"Why—why, Mr. Calhoun!" cried Mrs. Campbell in a shocked voice, "did you salt that mine on purpose?"

"You'd have thought so," he returned, "if you'd seen me packing the ore. It took me nigh onto two weeks."

Mrs. Campbell paused and gasped, but Wunpost met her gaze with a cold, unblinking stare. Her nice Scotch scruples were not for such as he, and if she crowded him too far he had an answer to her reproaches which would effectually reduce her to silence. But Billy knew that answer, and the reason for the gleam which played like heat-lightning in his eyes, and she hastened to stave off disaster.

"Oh, mother!" she protested, "now please don't talk seriously to him or he'll confess to almost anything. He told me a lot of stuff and I was dreadfully worried about it, but I found out he only did it to tease me. And besides, you know yourself that Mr. Eells did take advantage of us and trick us out of our mine—and if it hadn't been for that we could have built the road ourselves without being beholden to anybody."

"But Billy, child!" she chided, "just think what you're saying. Is it any excuse that others are dishonest? Well, I must say I'm surprised!"

"Oh, you're surprised, are you?" spoke up Wunpost, rising ponderously to his feet. "Well, if you don't like my style, just say so."

He reached for his hat and stood waiting for the answer, but Mrs. Campbell avoided the issue.

"It is not for us to judge our neighbors—the Bible says: Judge not, lest ye be judged—but I'm sorry, Mr. Calhoun, that you think so poorly of us as to boast of the deception you practised. He's no friend of us, this Judson Eells, but surely you cannot think it was aught but dishonest to sell him a salted mine. Vengeance is mine, saith the Lord, and because he took your property is no excuse for committing a crime."

"A *crime!*" repeated Wunpost, and turned to look at Billy, who hung her head regretfully. "Did you hear that?" he asked. "She says I'm a criminal! Well, I won't bother you folks any more. But before I go, Mrs. Campbell, I might as well tell you that these criminals sometimes come in danged handy. Suppose I'd buried that

181

ore in Happy Canyon, for instance, or over the summit in Hanaupah—where would the Campbell family be for a road? They wouldn't have one, *would* they? And this here Providence that you talk about would be distributing its rewards to others. But there's too many good people for the rewards to go around—that's why some of us get out and rustle. No, you want to be thankful that a criminal came along and took a flyer at being Providence himself; otherwise you'd be stuck with your mine on your hands— because I gave you that road, myself."

He started for the door and Mrs. Campbell let him go, for the revelation had left her thunderstruck. Never for a moment had she doubted that the sterling integrity of her husband had brought a special dispensation of Providence, and while her faith in Divine Providence was by no means shaken, she did begin to doubt the miracle. Perhaps, after all, this loud and boastful Wunpost had been more than an instrument of Providence—he might, in fact, have been a kindly but misguided friend, who had shaped his vengeance to serve their special needs. For he knew they needed the road and, since he could salt a crevice anywhere, he had located his mine up their canyon. And then Eells had jumped the mine and built the road, and— Well, really, after all, it was no more than right to go out and thank him for his kindness. He was wrong, of course, and led astray by angry passions; but Wilhelmina and he were friends and— She rose up and hurried out after him.

The blazing light in the heavens almost blinded her sight as she stepped out into the sun; and high up above the peaks, like cones of burnished metal, she saw two thundercaps, turning black at the base and mounting on the superheated air. There was the hush in the air which she had learned to associate with an explosion such as was about to take place, and she looked back anxiously, for her husband was up the canyon and the downpour might strike above Panamint. It was clouds such as these that had come together before to form the cloudburst which had isolated their mine, and though they now appeared daily she could never escape the fear that once more they would send down their floods. Every day they struck somewhere, and one more bone-dry canyon ran bank-high and spewed its refuse across the plain, and each time she had the feeling that their sins might be punished by another visitation from on high. But she only glanced back once, for Wunpost was packing and Billy was looking on hopelessly.

"Oh, Mr. Calhoun!" she called, "please don't go up the canyon now—there's a cloudburst forming above the peaks."

"I'll make it," he grumbled, cocking his eye at the clouds—and then he stopped and looked

183

again. "There went lightning," he said; "that's a mighty bad sign—they're stabbing out towards each other."

"Yes, I'm sure you'd better stay," she went on apologetically, "and please don't think you're not welcome. But oh! this heat is terrible—I'll have to go back—but Billy will stop and help you."

She raised her sunshade as if she were fleeing from a rain-storm and hastened back out of the sun; and Wunpost, after a minute of careful scrutiny, unpacked and squatted down in the shade.

"They're moving together," he said to Billy, "and see that lightning reaching out? This is going to bust the world open, somewhere. That's no cloudburst that's shaping up, it's a regular old waterspout; I know by the way she acts."

He settled back on his heels to await the outcome, and as the thunder began to roll he turned to his companion and shook his head in ominous silence. There were but two clouds in the sky, all the rest was blazing light; and these two clouds were moving slowly together, or rather, towards a common center. One came on from the southeast, the other from the west, and some invisible force seemed to be drawing them towards the peaks which marked the summit of the Panamints. The play of the lightning became almost constant, the rumbling rose to a tumult;

and then, as if caught by resistless hands, the two clouds rushed together. There was a flash of white light, a sudden blackening of the mass, and as Wunpost leapt up shouting a writhing funnel reached down as if feeling for the palpitating earth.

"There she goes!" he cried; "it's a waterspout, all right—but it ain't going to land near here."

He talked on, half to himself, as the great spiral reached and lengthened; and then he shouted again, for it had struck the ground, though where it was impossible to tell. The high rim of the canyon cut off all but the high peaks, and they could see nothing but the waterspout now; and it, as if stabilized by its contact with the earth, had turned into a long line of black. It was a column of falling water, and the two clouds, which had joined, seemed to be discharging their contents down a hole. They were sucked into the vortex, now turned an inky black, and their millions of tons of water were precipitated upon one spot, while all about the ground was left dry.

Wunpost knew what was happening, for he had seen it once before, and as he watched the rain descend he imagined the spot where it fell and the wreck which would follow its flood. For the Panamints are set on edge and shed rain like a roof, the water all flowing off at once; and when they strike a canyon, after rushing down the converging gulches, there is nothing that can

185

withstand their violence. Every canyon in the range, and in the Funeral Range beyond, and in Tin Mountain and the Grapevines to the north—every one of them had been swept by the floods from the heights and ripped out as clean as a sand-wash. And this waterspout, which had turned into a mighty cloudburst, would sweep one of them clean again. The question was—which one?

A breeze, rising suddenly, came up from the Sink and was sucked into the vortex above; the black line of the downfall turned lead-color and broadened out until it merged into the clouds above; and at last, as Wunpost lingered, the storm disappeared and the canyon took on the hush of heavy waiting. The sun blazed out as before, the fig-leaves hung down wilted; but the humidity was gone and the dry, oven-heat almost created the illusion of coolness.

"Well, I'm going," announced Wunpost, for the third or fourth time. "She must have come down away north."

"No—wait!" protested Billy, "why are you always in such a hurry? And perhaps the flood hasn't come yet."

"It'd be here," he answered, "been an hour, by my watch; and believe me, that old boy would be coming some. Excuse *me,* if it should hit into one end of a box canyon while I was coming up the other. My friends could omit the flowers."

"Well, why not stay, then?" she pouted anxiously; "you know Mother didn't mean anything. And perhaps Father will be down, to see if there was any damage done, and we could catch him first and explain."

"No explaining for me!" returned Wunpost, beginning to pack; "you can tell them whatever you want. And if your folks are too religious to use my old road maybe the Lord will send a cloudburst and destroy it. That's the way He always did in them old Bible stories—"

"You oughten to talk that way!" warned Wilhelmina soberly, "and besides, that's what made Mother angry. She isn't feeling well, and when you spoke slightingly of Divine Providence—"

"Well, I'm going," he said again, "before I begin to quarrel with *you*. But, oh say, I want to get that dog."

"Oh, it's too hot!" she protested, "let him stay under the house. He and Red are sleeping there together."

"No, I need him," he grumbled, "liable to be bushwhacked now, any time; and I want a dog to guard camp at night."

He started towards the house, still looking up the canyon, and at the gate he stopped dead and listened.

"What's that?" he asked, and glanced about wildly, but Billy only shook her head.

"I don't hear anything," she replied, turning listlessly away, "but I wish you wouldn't go."

"Well, maybe I won't," he answered grimly, "don't you hear that kind of rumble, up the canyon?"

She listened again, then rushed towards the house while Wunpost made a dash for the corral. The cloudburst was coming down their canyon.

CHAPTER XVII

THE ANSWER

THE rumbling up the canyon was hardly a noise; it was a tremulous shudder of earth and air like the grinding that accompanies an earthquake. But Wunpost knew, and the Campbells knew, what it meant and what was to follow; and as it increased to a growl they threw down the corral bars and rushed the stock up to the high ground. They waited, and Wunpost ran back to get his dog, and then the dammed waters broke loose. A great spray of yellow mud splashed out from Corkscrew Gorge and a piñon-trunk was snapped high into the air; and while all the earth trembled the dam of mud burst forth, forced on by the weight of backed-up waters. Then more trees came smashing through, followed by muddy tides of driftwood, and as suddenly the debacle ceased.

There was quiet, except for the hoarse rumble of boulders as they ground their way down through the Gorge; and for the muffled crack of submerged tree-trunks, straining and breaking beneath the ever-mounting jamb. It rose up and overflowed in a gush of turbid waters, rose still higher and overflowed again; and then it broke loose in a crash like imminent thunder—the

189

cloudburst had conquered the Gorge. It went through it and over it, spreading out on its sloping sides; and when the worst crush seemed over it washed higher yet and came through with an all-devouring surge. In a flash the whole creek-bed was a mass of mud and driftwood, which swashed about and swayed drunkenly on; and, as great tree-boles came battering through, the jamb broke abruptly and spewed out a sea of yellow water.

The fugitives climbed up higher, followed by the cat and dog, and the burros which had been left in the corrals; but the flood bore swiftly on, leaving the ranch unsullied by its burden of brush and mud. The jamb broke down again, letting out a second gush of water which crept up among the lower trees, but just as the Gorge opened up for the third time the flood-crest struck the lower gorge and stopped. Once more the trees and logs which had formed the jamb above bobbed and floated on the surface of a pond; and while the Campbells gazed and wept the turbid flood swung back swiftly, inundating their ranch with its mud.

First the orchard was overflowed then the garden above the road, then the corrals and the flowers by the gate; and as they ran about distracted the water crept up towards the house and out over the verdant alfalfa. But just when it seemed as if the whole ranch would be destroyed there was a smash from the lower point; the jamb went out, draining the waters quickly away and rushing on towards the Sink. The great mass of mud and boulders which had been brought down by the flood ceased to spread out and cover their fields, and as the millrace of waters continued to pour down the canyon it began to dig a new stream-bed in the débris. Then the thunder of its roaring subsided by degrees and by sundown the cloudburst was past.

Where the creek had been before there was a wider and deeper creek, its sides cumbered with huge boulders and tree-trunks; and the mixture of silt and gravel which formed its cut banks already had set like cement. It *was* cement, the same natural concrete which Nature combines everywhere on the desert—gravel and lime and bone-dry clay, sluiced and mixed by the passing cloudburst and piled up to set into pudding-stone. And all the mud which had overlaid the garden and orchard was setting like a concrete pavement. The ancient figs and peach-trees, half buried in the slime, rose up stiffly from the fertile soil beneath; and the Jail Canyon Ranch, once so flamboyantly green, was now shore-lined with a blotch of dirty gray. Only the alfalfa patch remained, and the house on the hill—everything else was either washed away or covered with gravel and dirt. And the road—it was washed away too.

Wunpost worked late and hard, shoveling the muck away from the trees and clearing a section of the corral; but not until Cole Campbell came down the next day was the Stinging Lizard road even mentioned. It was gone, they all knew that, and all their prayers and tears could not bring back one rock from its grade; and yet somehow Wunpost felt guilty, as if his impious words had brought down this disaster upon his friends. He rushed feverishly about in the blazing sun, trying to undo the most imminent damage; and Billy and Mrs. Campbell, half divining his futile regrets, went about their own tasks in silence. But when Campbell came down over the mountain-sheep trail and beheld what the cloudburst had done he spoke what came first into his mind.

"Ah, my road," he moaned, talking half to himself after the manner of the lonely and deaf, "and I let it lie idle six weeks! All my ore still sacked and waiting on the dump, and now my road is gone."

He bowed his head and gave way to tears, for he had lost ten years' work in a day, and then Mrs. Campbell forgot. She had remained silent before, not wishing to seem unkind, but now she spoke from her heart.

"It's a visitation!" she wailed; "the Lord has punished us for our sins. We should never have used the road."

"And why not?" demanded Campbell, rousing up from his brooding, and he saw Wunpost turning guiltily away. "Ah, I knew it!" he burst out; "I misdoubted it all the time, but you thought you could keep it from me. But when I came down from Panamint, to see where the waterspout had struck, and found it tearing in from Woodpecker Canyon, I said: 'It is the hand of God!' We had not come by our road quite honestly."

"No," sobbed Mrs. Campbell, "and I hate to say it, but I'm glad the road is destroyed. What you built we came by honestly, but the rest was obtained by fraud, and now it has all been destroyed. You have worked long and hard, Cole, and I'm sorry this had to happen; but God is not mocked, we know that. I tried to keep it from you, and to keep myself from knowing; but he told me himself that he salted the mine on purpose, so that Eells would build us a road!"

"Aha!" nodded Campbell, and looked out from under his eyebrows at the man who had befriended him by fraud. But he was a man of few words, and his silence spoke for him— Wunpost scuffled his feet and withdrew.

"Well I'm going," he announced to Billy as he threw on his packs; "this is getting too rough for me. So I crabbed the whole play, eh, and fetched that cloudburst down Woodpecker? And it washed out your father's road! It's a wonder

193

Divine Providence didn't ketch *me* up the canyon, and wipe me off the footstool, too!"

"Perhaps He spared you," suggested Billy, whose eyes were big with awe, "so you could repent and be forgiven of your sins."

"I bet ye!" scoffed Wunpost; "but you can't tell *me* that God Almighty was steering that waterspout. It just hit in Woodpecker Canyon, same as one hit Hanaupah last week and another one washed out down below. They're falling every day, but I'm going up into them hills, and do you reckon one will drop on me? Don't you think it—God Almighty has got more important business than following me around through the hills. I'm going to take my little dog, so I'll be sure to have Good Luck; and if I don't come back you'll know somebody has got me, that's all."

He tightened his lash ropes viciously, mounted his horse and took the lead, followed by Old Walker and the other mules, packed; and when he whistled for Good Luck, to Billy's surprise the little terrier went bounding off after him. She waved at him furtively and tried to toll him back, but his devotion to his master was still just as strong as it had been when he had adopted him in Los Angeles. When he had been prostrated by the heat he had stayed with Billy gladly, but now that he was strong and accustomed to the climate he raced along after

194

the mules. Wunpost looked back and grinned, then he reached down a hand and swooped his dog up into the saddle.

"You can't steal him!" he hooted, and Billy bit her lip, for she thought she had weaned him from his master. And Wunpost—she had thought he was tamed to her hand, but he too had gone off and left her. He was still as wild and ruthless as on the day they had first met, when he had been chasing Dusty Rhodes with a stone; and now he was heading off into the high places he was so fond of, to play hide-and-seek with his pursuers. Several had come up already, ostensibly to view the ruin but undoubtedly to keep Wunpost in sight; and if he continued his lawless strife she doubted if the good Lord would preserve him, as He had from the cloudburst.

Time and again he had mounted to go and each time she had held him back, for she had sensed some imminent disaster; and now, as he rode off, she felt the prompting again to run after him and call him back. But he would not come back, he was headstrong and unrepentant, making light of what others held sacred; and as she watched him out of sight something told her again that he was going out to meet his doom. Some great punishment was hanging over him, to chastise him for his sins and bring him, perhaps, to repentance; but she could no more stop his going, or turn him aside from his purpose, than she could control the rush of a cloudburst. He was like a force of nature—a rude, fighting creature who beat down opposition as the flood struck down bushes, rushing on to seek new worlds to conquer.

CHAPTER XVIII

A LESSON

THE heat-wave, which had made even the desert-dwellers pant, came to an end with the Jail Canyon waterspout; the nights became bearable, the rocks cooled off and the sun ceased to strike through men's clothes. But there was one, still clinging to her faded bib-overalls, who took no joy in the blessed release. Wilhelmina was worried, for the sightseers from Blackwater had disappeared as soon as Wunpost rode away; and now, two days later, his dog had come back, meeching and whining and licking its feet. Good Luck had left Wunpost and returned to the ranch, where he was sure of food and a friend; but now that he was fed he begged and whimpered uneasily and watched every move that she made. And every time that she started towards the trail where Wunpost had ridden away he barked and ran eagerly ahead. Billy stood it until noon, then she caught up Tellurium and rode off after the dog.

He led up the trail, where he had run so often before, but over the ridge he turned abruptly downhill and Billy refused to follow. Wunpost certainly had taken the upper trail, for there were his tracks leading on; and the dog, after all, had no notion of leading her to his master. He was still young and inexperienced, though with that thoroughbred smartness which set him apart from the ordinary cur; but when she made as though to follow he cut circles with delight and ran along enticingly in front of her. So Billy rode after him, and at the foot of the hill she found mule-tracks heading off north. Wunpost had made a wide detour and come back, probably at night, to throw off his pursuers and start fresh; but as she followed the tracks she found where several horse-tracks had circled and cut into his trail. She picked up Good Luck, who was beginning to get footsore, and followed the mule-tracks at a lope.

Near the mouth of the canyon they struck out over the mud, which the cloudburst had spread out for miles, but now they were across and going down the slope which a thousand previous floods had laid. Ahead lay Warm Springs, where the Indians sometimes camped; but the trail cut out around them and headed for Fall Canyon, the next big valley to the north. She rode on steadily, her big pistol that Wunpost had once borrowed now back in its accustomed place; and the fact that she had failed to tell her parents of her intentions did not keep her from taking up the hunt. Wunpost was in trouble, and she knew it; and now she was on her way, either to find him or to make sure he was safe.

The trail up Fall Canyon twists and winds among wash boulders, over cut-banks and up sandy gulches; but at the mouth of the canyon it plunges abruptly into willow-brush and leads on up the bed of a dry creek. Once more the steep ridges closed in and made deep gorges, the hillsides were striped with blues and reds; and along the ancient trail there were tunnels and dumps of rock where prospectors had dug in for gold. There were dog tracks in the mud showing where Good Luck had come down, and she knew Wunpost must be up there somewhere; but when she came upon a mule, lying down under his pack, she started and clutched at her gun. The mule jumped up noisily and ran smashing through the willows, then turned with a terrifying snort; and as she drew rein and stopped Good Luck sprang to the ground and rushed silently off up the canyon.

Billy followed along cautiously, driving the snorting mule before her and looking for something she feared to find. A buzzard rose up slowly, flopping awkwardly to clear the canyon wall, and her heart leapt once and stood still. There in the open lay Wunpost's horse, its sharp-shod feet in the air, and there was a bullet-hole through its side. She stopped and looked about, at the ridge, at the sky, at the knife-like gash ahead; and then she set her teeth and spurred up the canyon to where the dog had set up a yapping.

He was standing by a tunnel at the edge of the creek, wagging his tail and waiting expectantly; and when she came in sight he dashed half-way to meet her and turned back to the hole in the hill. She rode up to its mouth, her eyes straining into the darkness, her breath coming in short, quick gasps; and Tellurium, advancing slowly, suddenly flew back and snorted as a voice came out from the depths.

"Hello, there!" it hailed; "say, bring me a drink of water. This is Calhoun—I'm shot in the leg."

"Well, what are you hiding in there for?" burst out Billy as she dismounted; "why don't you crawl out and get some yourself?"

Now that she knew he was alive a swift impatience swept over her, an unreasoning anger that he had caused her such a fright, and as she unslung her canteen and started for the tunnel her stride was almost vixenish. But when she found him stretched out on the bare, uneven rocks with one bloody leg done up in bandages, she knelt down suddenly and held out the canteen, which he seized and almost drained at one drink.

"Fine! Fine!" he smacked; "began to think you wasn't coming—did you bring along that medicine I wrote for?"

"Why, what medicine?" exclaimed Billy. "No, I didn't find a note—Good Luck must have lost it on the way."

"Well, never mind," he said; "just catch one of my mules and we'll go back to the ranch after dark."

"But who shot you?" clamored Billy, "and what are you in here for? We'll start back home right now!"

"No we won't!" he vetoed; "there's some Injuns up above there and they're doing their best to git me. You can't see 'em—they're hid—but when I showed myself this noon some dastard took a crack at me with his Winchester. Did you happen to bring along a little grub?"

"Why, yes," assented Billy, and went out in a kind of trance—it was so unreasonable, so utterly absurd. Why should Indians be watching to shoot down Wunpost when he had always been friendly with them all? And for that matter, why should anyone desire to kill him—that certainly could never lead them to his mine. The men who had come to the ranch were Blackwater prospectors—she knew them all by sight—and if it was they who had followed him she was absolutely sure that Wunpost had started the fight. She stepped out into the dazzling sunshine and looked up at the ridges that rose tier by tier above her, but she had no fear either of white men or Indians, for she had done nothing to make them her enemies. Whoever they were, she knew she was safe—but Wunpost was hiding in a cave. All his bravado gone, he was afraid to venture out even to wet his parched throat at the creek.

"What were you doing?" she demanded when she had given him her lunch, and Wunpost reared up at the challenge.

"I was riding along that trail," he answered defiantly, "and I wasn't doing a thing. And then a bullet came down and got me through the leg— I didn't even hear the shot. All I know is I was riding and the next thing I knew I was down and my horse was laying on my leg. I got out from under him somehow and jumped over into the brush, and I've been hiding here ever since. But it's Lynch that's behind it—I know that for a certainty—he's hired some of these Injuns to bushwhack me."

"Have you seen them?" she asked unbelievingly.

"No, and I don't need to," he retorted. "I guess I know Injuns by this time. That's just the way they work—hide out on some ridge and pot a man when he goes by. But they're up there, I know it, because one of them took a shot at me this noon—and anyhow I can just *feel* 'em!"

"Well, *I* can't," returned Billy, "and I don't believe they're there; and if they are they won't hurt me. They all know me too well, and we've always been good to them. I'm going up to catch your mules."

"No, look out!" warned Wunpost; "them devils are treacherous, and I wouldn't put it past 'em to

202

shoot you. But you wait till I get this leg of mine fixed and I'll make some of 'em hard to ketch!"

"Now you see what you get," burst out Billy heartlessly, "for taking Mr. Lynch to Poison Spring. I'm sorry you're shot, but when you get well I hope this will be a lesson to you. Because if it wasn't for your dog, and me running away from home, you never would get away from here alive."

"Well, for cripes' sake!" roared Wunpost, "don't you think I know that now? What's the use of rubbing it in? And you're dead right it'll be a lesson—I'll ride the ridges, after this, and the next time I'll try to shoot first. But you go up the canyon and throw the packs off them mules and bring me Old Walker to ride. I ain't crippled; I'm all right, but this leg is sure hurting me and I believe I'll take a chance. Saddle him up and we'll start for the ranch."

Billy stepped out briskly, half smiling at his rage and at the straits to which his anger had brought him; but when she heard his heavy groaning as she helped him into the saddle her woman's heart was touched. After all he was just a child, a big reckless boy, still learning the hard lessons of life; and it had certainly been treacherous for the assassin to shoot him without even giving him a chance. She rode close beside him as they went down the canyon, to protect him from possible bullets; and if Wunpost divined her purpose it did not prevent him from keeping her between him and the ridge. The wound and the long wait had shattered his nerves and made him weak and querulous, and he cursed softly whenever he hit his sore leg; but back at the ranch his spirits revived and he insisted upon going on to Blackwater.

Cole Campbell had cleaned his wound and drenched it well with dilute carbolic, but though it was clean and would heal in a few days, Wunpost demanded to be taken to town. He was restless and uneasy in the presence of these people, whose standards were so different from his own; but behind it all there was some hidden purpose which urged him on to Los Angeles. It was shown in the set lips, the stern brooding stare and his impatience with his motion-impeding leg; but to Billy it was shown most by his oblivious glances and the absence of all proper gratitude. She had done a brave deed in following his dog back and in rescuing him from the bullets of his enemies, but when she drew near and tried to engage him in conversation his answers were mostly in monosyllables. Only once did he rouse up, and that was when she said that Lynch was even with him now, and the look in his eyes gave Billy to understand that he was not even with Lynch. That was it—he was unrepentant, he was brooding revenge, he was planning even more desperate deeds; but he would not tell her, or even admit that he was worried about anything but his leg. It was hurting him, he said, and he wanted a good doctor to see it before it grew worse; but when he went away he avoided her eye and Billy ran off and wept.

CHAPTER XIX

TAINTED MONEY

A MONTH passed by and the haze above the Sink lifted its shroud and revealed the mountains beyond; the soft blues and pinks crept back into the distance and the shadowy canyons were filled with royal purple. At dawn a silver radiance rose and glowed along the east and the sunsets stained the west with orange and gold; there was wine in the cool air, and when the night wind came up the prospectors crouched over their fires. The first October storm put a crown on Telescope Peak and tipped the lesser Panamints with snow, but still Wilhelmina waited and Wunpost did not return from his mysterious trip "inside."

The time was not ripe for his notable revenge and he had forgotten Jail Canyon and her. Yet at last she saw his dust, and as she watched him through her glasses something told her that his thoughts were not of her. He was on his way, either seeking after gold or searching out the means of revenge; and if he came that way it was to find his dog and mules and not to make love to her. Their ranch was merely his half-way house, a place to feed his animals and leave them when he went away; and she was only a child, to be noticed like a fond dog, but not to be taken seriously. Billy put up her glasses and went back to the house, and when he arrived she was a woman. Her hair was done up gracefully, her nimble limbs were confined in skirts; and she smiled at him demurely, as if her mind was far away and he had recalled her from maidenly dreams.

"Well, well!" exclaimed Wunpost as he limped up to the house and discovered her on the shady front porch; "where's the trusty bib-overalls and all? What's the matter—is it Sunday, or did you see my dust? Say, you don't look right without them curls!"

"We're thinking of moving away," she explained quite truthfully, "and I can't wear overalls then."

"Moving away!" cried Wunpost; "why, where were you thinking of going to? Has your father given up on his road?"

"Well, no—or that is, he's working on a trail to pack down the ore he had sacked. And after that's shipped, if it pays him what it ought, we're going to move inside."

"Oh," observed Wunpost and sat down on the porch, where he rumpled his hair reflectively. "Say," he said at last, "I've got a little roll—what's the matter if I build the road?"

"Shh!" she hissed, moving over and speaking low; "don't you know that Mother wouldn't hear to it? And poor Father, he feels awful bad."

"No, but look," he protested, "you folks have been my friends, and I owe you for taking care of my mules. I'd be glad to advance the money to put in an aerial tramway and you could pay it back out of the ore. That's the kind of road you want, one that will never wash out, and I know where you can get one cheap. There's one down by Goler that you can buy for almost nothing—I stopped and looked it over, coming up. And all you have to do, after you once get it installed, is to feed your ore into the buckets and send them down the canyon and the empties will come up with your supplies. It's automatic—works itself, and can't get out of order—just a long, double cable, swinging down from point to point and supplying its own power by gravity. Some class to that, and I tell you what I'll do—I'll lend the money to *you!*"

"No!" she said as he reached down into his pocket, and she gazed at him reproachfully.

"What do you mean?" he asked after a minute of puzzled silence, and she shook her head and pointed towards the house. Then she rose up quietly and led off down the path where the hollyhocks were still in full bloom.

"You know what I mean," she said at the gate; "have you forgotten about the cloudburst?"

"Why, no," he returned; "you don't mean to say—"

"Yes, I do," she replied, "they think your

money is accursed. Father says you didn't come by it honestly."

"Oh, he does, eh?" sulked Wunpost; "and what do you think about it?"

"I think the same," she answered promptly and looked him straight in the eye.

"Well, well," he began with a sardonic smile, and then he thrust out his lip. "All right, kid," he said, "excuse me for living, but I wouldn't be that good if I could. It takes all the roar out of life. Now here I came back with some money in my pocket, to make you a little present, and the first thing you hand me is this: 'My money ain't come by honestly.' Well, that's the end of the present."

He shrugged his shoulders and waited, but Billy made no reply.

"I went up into the hills," he went on at last, "and discovered a vein of gold—nobody had ever owned it before. And I dug it out and showed the ore to Eells and asked him if he thought it was his. No, he said he couldn't claim it. Well, I took it to Los Angeles and sold it to a jeweler and here's the money he paid me for it—don't you think that money is honest?"

He drew out a sheaf of bills and flicked the ends temptingly, but Billy shook her head.

"No," she said, "because you don't dare to show the place where you claim you dug up that gold and you told Mr. Eells you *stole* it!"

"Heh, heh!" chuckled Wunpost, "you keep right up with me, kid. Don't reckon I can give you any present. I was just thinking you might like to take a trip to Los Angeles, and see the bright lights and all—taking your mother along, and so forth—but it's Jail Canyon for you, for life. If this thousand dollar bill that you earned by saving my life is nothing but tainted money, all I can do is to tender a vote of thanks. It must be fierce to have a Scotch conscience."

"You mind your own business," answered Billy shortly, and brushed away a furtive tear. A trip to Los Angeles—and new clothes and everything— and she really had earned the money! Yes, she had saved his life and enabled him to come back to dig up some more hidden gold. But it was stolen, and there was an end to it—she turned away abruptly, but he caught her by the hand.

"Say, listen, kid," he said; "I may not be an angel, but I never go back on a friend. Now you tell me what you want and, no matter what it is, I'll go out and get it for you—honestly. You're the best friend I've got—and you sure look swell, dressed up in them women's clothes—but I want you to have a good time. I want you to go inside and see the world, and go to the theaters and all, but how'm I going to slip you the money?"

Billy laughed, rather hysterically, and then she turned grave and her eyes looked far away.

"All I want," she said at last, "is a road up Father's canyon—and I know he won't accept it from you. So let's talk about something else. Are you going back to your mine?"

He sighed, then glanced up at the ridge and nodded his head mysteriously.

"There's somebody after me," he said at last. "They follow me up now, every place. In town it's detectives, and out here on the desert it's Pisen-face Lynch and his gang. But I don't mind them—I'm looking for that feller that shot me in the leg last month. It wasn't Lynch—I've had him traced—and it wasn't none of those Shooshonnies; but there's some feller in these hills that's out after my scalp and I've come back to get him. And when I find him, kid, I'll light a fire under him that'll burn 'im off the face of the earth. I'm going to kill him, by grab, the same as I would a rattlesnake; I'm going to—"

"Oh, please don't talk that way!" broke in Wilhelmina impatiently, "it gives people a bad impression. There isn't a man in Blackwater that isn't firmly convinced that you're nothing but a bag of hot air. Well, I don't care—that's just what they said!"

"Ahhr!" scoffed Wunpost, "them Blackwater stiffs. They're jealous, that's what's the matter."

"No, but don't talk that way," she pleaded. "It turns folks against you. Even Father and Mother

211

have noticed it. You're always telling of the big things you're going to do—"

"Well, don't I *do* 'em?" he demanded. "What did I ever say I'd do that I didn't make good, in the end? Don't you think I'm going to get this bad *hombre*—this feller that's following me through the hills? Well, I'll tell you what I'll do. If I don't bring you his hair inside of a month—you can have my mine and everything. But I'm going to *git* him, see? I'm going to toll him across the Valley, where he'll have to come out into the open, and when I ketch him I'm going to scalp him. He's nothing but a low-down, murdering assassin that old Eells or somebody has hired—"

"Oh, *please!*" she protested and his eyes opened big before they closed down in a sudden scowl.

"Well, I'll show you," he said and packed and rode off in silence.

CHAPTER XX

THE WAR EAGLE

SINCE a bullet from nowhere had shot him through the leg, Wunpost had learned a new fear of the hills. Before, they had been his stamping-ground, the "high places" he was so boastful of; but now they became imbued with a malign personality, all the more fearful because it was unknown. With painstaking care he had checked up on Pisen-face Lynch, to determine if it was he who had ambushed him; but Lynch had established a perfect alibi—in fact, it was almost too good. He had been right in Blackwater during all the trouble, although now he was out in the hills; and an Indian whom Wunpost had sent on a scout reported that the Shoshones had no knowledge of the shooting. They, too, had become aware of the strange presence in the hills, though none of them had really seen it, and their women were afraid to go out after the piñon-nuts for fear of being caught and stolen.

The prowler was no renegade Shoshone, for his kinsmen would know about him, and yet Wunpost had a feeling it was an Indian. And he had another hunch—that the Indian was employed by Eells and Pisen-face Lynch. For,

213

despite Wilhelmina's statement, there was one man in Blackwater who did not consider him a bag of hot air. Judson Eells took him seriously, so seriously, in fact, that he was spending thousands of dollars on detectives; and Wunpost knew for a certainty that there was a party in the hills, waiting and watching to trail him to his mine. His departure from Los Angeles had been promptly reported, and Lynch and several others had left town—which was yet another reason why Wunpost quit the hills and went north over the Death Valley Trail.

Life had suddenly become a serious affair to the man who had discovered the Willie Meena, and as he neared that mine he veered off to the right and took the high ground to Wild Rose. Yet he could not but observe that the mine was looking dead, and rumor had it that the paystreak had failed. The low-grade was still there and Eells was still working it; but out on the desert and sixty miles from the railroad it could hardly be expected to pay. No, Judson Eells was desperate, for he saw his treasure slipping as the Wunpost had slipped away before; it was slipping through his fingers and he grasped at any straw which might help him to find the Sockdolager. It was the curse of the Panamints that the veins all pinched out or ran into hungry ore; and for the second time, when he had esteemed himself rich, he had found the bottom of the hole. He had built roads and piped water and set up a mill and settled down to make his pile; and then, with that strange fatality which seemed to pursue him, he had seen his profits fail. The assays had shown that his pay-ore was limited and that soon the Willie Meena must close, and now he was taking the last of his surplus and making a desperate fight for the Sockdolager.

Half the new mine was his, according to law, and since Wunpost had dared him to do his worst he was taking him at his word. And Wunpost at last was getting scared, though not exactly of Eells. For, since he alone knew the location of his mine, and no one could find it if he were dead, it stood to reason that Eells would never kill him, or give orders to his agents to kill. But what those agents were doing while they were out in the field, and how far they would respect his wishes, was something about which Eells knew no more than Wunpost, if, in fact, he knew as much. For Wunpost had a limp in his good right leg which partially conveyed the answer, and it was his private opinion that Lynch had gone bad and was out in the hills to kill him. Hence his avoidance of the peaks, and even the open trail; and the way he rode into water after dark.

There were Indians at Wild Rose, Shooshon Johnny and his family on their way to Furnace

Creek for the winter; but though they were friendly Wunpost left in the night and camped far out on the plain. It was the same sandy plain over which he had fled when he had led Lynch to Poison Spring, and as he went on at dawn Wunpost felt the first vague misgivings for his part in that unfortunate affair. It had lost him a lot of friends and steeled his enemies against him—Lynch no longer was working by the day—and sooner or later it was likely to cost him dear, for no man can win all the time. Yet he had thrown down the gauntlet, and if he weakened now and quit his name would be a byword on the desert. And besides he had made his boast to Wilhelmina that he would come back with his assailant's back hair.

It was a matter of pride with John C. Calhoun that, for all his wild talk, he never made his brag without trying to live up to his word. He had stated in public that he was going to break Eells, and he fully intended to do so; and his promise to get Lynch and Phillip F. Lapham was never out of his mind; but this assassin, this murderer, who had shot him without cause and then crawled off through the boulders like a snake—Wunpost had schemed night and day from the moment he was hit to bring the sneaking miscreant to book. He had some steel-traps in his packs which might serve to good purpose if he could once get the man-hunter on his trail; and he still fondly hoped to lure him over into Death Valley, where he would have to come out of the hills.

No man could cross that Valley without leaving his tracks, for there were alkali flats for miles; and when, in turn, Wunpost wished to cover his own trail, there was always the Devil's Playground. There, whenever the wind blew, the great sandhills were on the move, covering up and at the same time laying bare; and when a sand storm came on he could lose his tracks half an hour after they were made. It was a big country, and wild, no man lived there for sixty miles—they could fight it out, alone.

From Emigrant Spring, where he camped after dark, Wunpost rode out before dawn and was well clear of the hills before it was light enough to shoot. The broad bulwark of Tucki Mountain, rising up on his right, might give a last shelter to his enemy; but now he was in the open with Emigrant Wash straight ahead and Death Valley lying white beyond. And over beyond that, like a wall of layer cake, rose the striated buttresses of the Grapevines. Wunpost passed down over the road up which the Nevada rush had come when he had made his great strike at Black Point; and as he rollicked along on his fast-walking mule, with the two pack-animals following behind, something rose up within him to tell him the world was good and that a lucky star was leading him on.

He was heading across the Valley to the Grapevine Range, and the hateful imp of evil which had dogged him through the Panamints would have to come down and leave a trail. And once he found his tracks Wunpost would know who he was fighting, and he could govern himself accordingly. If it was an Indian, well and good; if it was Lynch, still well and good; but no man can be brave when he is fighting in the dark or fleeing from an unseen hand. From their lookouts on the heights his enemies could see him traveling and trace him with their glasses all day; but when night fell they would lose him, and then someone would have to descend and pick up his trail in the sands.

Wunpost camped that evening at Surveyor's Well, a trench-hole dug down into the Sink, and after his mules had eaten their fill of salt-grass he packed up again and pushed on to the east. From the stinking alkali flat with its mesquite clumps and sacaton, he passed on up an interminable wash; and at daylight he was hidden in the depths of a black canyon which ended abruptly behind him. There was no way to reach him, or even see where he was hid, except by following up the canyon; and before he went to sleep Wunpost got out his two bear-traps and planted them hurriedly in the trail. Then, retiring into a cave, he left Good Luck on guard and slept until late in the day. But nothing stirred down the trail, his watch-dog was silent—he was hidden from all the world.

That evening just at dusk he went back down the trail and set his bear-traps again, but not even a prowling fox came along in the night to spring their cruel jaws. The canyon was deserted and the water-hole where he drank was unvisited except by his mules. These he had penned in above him by a fence of brush and ropes and hobbled them to make doubly sure; but in the morning they were there, waiting to receive their bait of grain as if Tank Canyon was their customary home. Another day dragged by and Wunpost began to fidget and to watch the unscalable peaks, but no Indian's head appeared to draw a slug from his rifle and again the night passed uneventfully. He spent the third day in a fury, pacing up and down his cave, and at nightfall he packed up and was gone.

Three days was enough to wait on the man who had shot him down from the heights and, now that he thought of it, he was taking a great deal for granted when he set his big traps in the trail. In the first place, he was assuming that the man was still there, after a lapse of six weeks and more; and in the second place that he was bold enough, or so obsessed by blood-lust, that he would follow him across Death Valley; whereas as a matter of fact, he knew nothing whatever about him except that he had shot him in the leg.

His aim had been good but a little too low, which is unusual when shooting down hill, and that might argue him a white man; but his hiding had been better, and his absolute patience, and that looked more like an Indian. But whoever he was, it was taking too much for granted to think that he would walk into a trap. What Wunpost wanted to know, and what he was about to find out, was whether his tracks had been followed.

He left Tank Canyon after dark, driving his pack-mules before him to detect any possible ambush; and in his nest on the front pack Good Luck stood up like a sentinel, eager to scent out the lurking foe. For the past day and night Good Luck had been uneasy, snuffing the wind and growling in his throat, but the actions of his master had been cause enough for that, for he responded to Wunpost's every mood. And Wunpost was as jumpy as a cat that has been chased by a dog, he practised for hours on the draw-and-shoot; and whenever he dismounted he dragged his rifle with him to make sure he would do it in a pinch. He was worried but not frightened and when he came free from the canyon he headed for Surveyor's Well.

Someone had been there before him, perhaps even that very night, for water had been splashed about the hole; but whoever it was, was gone. Wunpost studied the unshod horse-track, then he began to cut circles in the snow-white alkali and at last he sat down to await the dawn. There was something eerie about this pursuit, if pursuit it was, for while the horse had been watered from the bucket at the well, its rider had not left a track. Not a heel-mark, not a nail-point, and the last of the water had been dropped craftily on the spot where he had mounted. That was enough—Wunpost knew he had met his match. He watered his mules again, rode west into the mesquite brush and at sun-up he was hid for the day.

Where three giant mesquite trees, their tops reared high in the air and their trunks banked up with sand, sprawled together to make a natural barricade, Wunpost unpacked his mules and tied them there to browse while he climbed to the top of a mound. The desert was quite bare as far as he could see—no horseman came or went, every distant trail was empty, the way to Tank Canyon was untrod. And yet somewhere there must be a man and a horse—a very ordinary horse, such as any man might have, and a man who wiped out his tracks. Wunpost lay there a long time, sweeping the washes with his glasses, and then a shadow passed over him and was gone. He jumped and a glossy raven, his head turned to one side, gave vent to a loud, throaty *quawk!* His mate followed behind him, her wings rustling noisily, her beady eye fixed on his camp, and Wunpost looked up and cursed back at them.

If the ravens on the mountain had made out his

hiding-place and come down from their crags to look, what was to prevent this man who smoothed out his tracks from detecting his hidden retreat? Wunpost knew the ravens well, for no man ever crossed Death Valley without hearing the whish of black wings, but he wondered now if this early morning visit did not presage disaster to come. What the ravens really sought for he knew all too well, for he had seen their knotted tracks by dead forms; yet somehow their passage conjured up thoughts in his brain which had never disturbed him before. They were birds of death, rapacious and evil-bringing, and they had cast their boding shadows upon him.

The dank coolness of the morning gave place to ardent midday before he crept down and gave up his watch, but as he crouched beneath the trees another shadow passed over him and cast a slow circle through the brush. It was a pair of black eagles, come down from the Panamints to throw a fateful circle above *him,* and in all his wanderings it had never happened before that an eagle had circled his camp. A superstitious chill made Wunpost shudder and draw back, for the Shoshones had told him that the eagles loved men's battles and came from afar to watch. They had learned in the old days that when one war-party followed another there would later be feasting and blood; and now, when one man followed another across the desert, they came down from their high cliffs to look. Wunpost scrambled to his hillock and watched their effortless flight; and they swung to the north, where they circled again, not far from the spot where he was hid. Here was an omen indeed, a sign without fail, for below where they circled his enemy was hiding—or slipping up through the brush to shoot.

We can all stand so much of superstitious fear and then the best nerves must crack—Wunpost saddled his mules and struck out due south, turning off into the "self-rising ground." Here in bloated bubbles of salt and poisonous niter the ground had boiled up and formed a brittle crust, like dough made of self-rising flour. It was a dangerous place to go, for at uncertain intervals his mules caved through to their hocks, but Wunpost did not stop till he had crossed to the other side and put ten miles of salt-flats behind him. He was haunted by a fear of something he could not name, of a presence which pursued him like a devil; but as he stopped and looked back the hot curses rushed to his lips and he headed boldly for the mouth of Tank Canyon.

CHAPTER XXI

A LOCK OF HAIR

IT is no disgrace to flee the unknown, for Nature has made that an instinct; but the will to overcome conquers even this last of fears and steels a man's nerves to face anything. The heroes of antiquity set their lances against dragons and creatures that belched forth flame and smoke—brave Perseus slew the Gorgon, and Jason the brass-hooved bulls, and St. George and many another slew his "worm." But the dragons are all dead or driven to the depths of the sea, whence they rise up to chill men's blood; and those who conquer now fight only their memory, passed down in our fear of the unknown. And Perseus and Jason had gods and sorceresses to protect them, but Wunpost turned back alone.

He entered Tank Canyon just as the sun sank in the west; and there at its entrance he found horse-tracks, showing dimly among the rocks. His enemy had been there, a day or two before, but he too had feared the unknown. He had gazed into that narrow passageway and turned away, to wait at Surveyor's Well for his coming. And Wunpost had come, but the eagles had saved him to give battle once more on his own ground. Tank Canyon was his stronghold, inaccessible from behind, cut off from the sides by high walls; and the evil one who pursued him must now brave its dark depths or play an Indian game and wait.

Wunpost threw off his packs and left his mules to fret while he ran back to plant the huge traps. They were not the largest size that would break a man's leg, but yet large enough to hold their victim firm against all the force he could exert. Their jaws spread a good foot and two powerful springs lurked beneath to give them a jump; and once the blow was struck nothing could pry those teeth apart but the clamps, which were operated by screws. A man caught in such a trap would be doomed to certain death if no one came to his aid and Wunpost's lips curled ferociously as he rose up from his knees and regarded his cunning handiwork. His traps were set not far apart, in the two holes he had dug before, and covered with the greatest care; but one was in the trail, where a man would naturally step, and the other was out in the rocks. A bush, pulled carelessly down, stuck out from the bank like a fragile but compelling hand; and Wunpost knew that the prowler would step around it by instinct, which would throw him into the trap.

The night was black in Tank Canyon and only a pathway of stars showed the edge of the boxed-in walls; it was black and very silent, for not a mouse was abroad, and yet Wunpost and his dog could not sleep. A dozen times before midnight Good Luck leapt up growling and bestrode his master's form, and at last he rushed out barking, his voice rising to a yell as he paused and listened through the silence. Wunpost lay in bed and waited, then rose cautiously up and peered from the mouth of the cave. A pale moon was shining on the jagged rocks above and there was a grayness that foretold the dawn, but the bottom of Tank Canyon was still dark as a pocket and he went back to wait for the day. Good Luck came back whining, and a growl rumbled in his throat—then he leapt up again and Wunpost felt his own hair rise, for a wail had come through the night. He slapped Good Luck into silence and listened again—and it came, a wild, animal-like cry. Yet it was the voice of a man and Wunpost sprang to his feet all a-tremble to gaze on his catch.

"I've got him!" he chuckled and drew on his boots; then tied up the dog and slipped out into the night.

The dawn had come when he rose up from behind a boulder and strained his eyes in the uncertain light, and where the trap had been there was now a rocking form which let out hoarse grunts of pain. It rose up suddenly and as the head came in view Wunpost saw that his pursuer was an Indian. His hair was long and cut off straight above the shoulders in the old-time Indian silhouette; but this buck was no

226

Shoshone, for they have given up the breech-clout and he wore a cloth about his hips.

"H'lo!" he hailed and Wunpost ducked back for he did not trust his guest. He was the man, beyond a doubt, who had shot him from the ridge; and such a man would shoot again. So he dropped down and lay silent, listening to the rattle of the huge chain and the vicious clash of the trap, and the Indian burst out scolding.

"Whassa mala!" he gritted, "my foot get caught in trap. You come fixum—fixum quick!"

Wunpost rose up slowly and peered out through a crack and he caught the gleam of a gun.

"You throw away that gun!" he returned from behind the boulder and at last he heard it clatter among the rocks. "Now your pistol!" he ordered, but the Indian burst out angrily in his guttural native tongue. What he said could only be guessed from his scolding tone of voice; but after a sullen pause he dropped back into English, this time complaining and insolently defiant.

"You shut up!" commanded Wunpost suddenly rising above his rock and covering the Indian with his gun, "and throw away that pistol or I'll kill you!"

The Indian reared up and faced him, then reached inside his waistband and threw a wicked gun into the dirt. He was grinding his teeth with pain, like a gopher in a trap, and his brows were drawn down in a fierce scowl; but Wunpost only laughed as he advanced upon him slowly, his gun held ready to shoot.

"Don't like it, eh?" he taunted, "well, I didn't like *this* when you up and shot me through the leg."

He slapped his leg and the Indian seemed to understand—or perhaps he misunderstood; his hand leapt like a flash to a butcher-knife in his moccasin-leg and Wunpost jumped as it went past his ribs. Then a silence fell, in which the fate of a human life hung on the remnant of what some people call pity, and Wunpost's trigger-finger relaxed. But it was not pity, it was just an age-old feeling against shooting a man in a trap. Or perhaps it was pride and the white man's instinct not to foul his clean hands with butcher's blood. Wunpost wanted to kill him but he stepped back instead and looked him in the eye.

"You rattlesnake-eyed dastard!" he hissed between his teeth and the Indian began to beg. Wunpost listened to him coldly, his eyes bulging with rage, and then he backed off and sat down.

"Who you working for?" he asked and as the Indian turned glum he rolled a cigarette and waited. The jaws of the steel-trap had caught him by the heel, stabbing their teeth through into the flesh, and in spite of his stoicism the Indian rocked back and forth and his little eyes glinted with the agony. Yet he would not talk and

Wunpost went off and left him, after gathering up his guns and the knife. There was something about that butcher-knife and the way it was flung which roused all the evil in Wunpost's heart and he meditated darkly whether to let the Indian go or give him his just deserts. But first he intended to wring a confession from him, and he left him to rattle his chain.

Wunpost cooked a hasty breakfast and fed and saddled his mules and then, as the Indian began to shout for help, he walked down and glanced at him inquiringly.

"You let me go!" ordered the Indian, drawing himself up arrogantly and shaking the coarse hair from his eyes, and Wunpost laughed disdainfully.

"Who are you?" he demanded, "and what you doing over here? I know them buckskin *tewas*—you're an Apache!"

"*Sí*—Apache!" agreed the Indian. "I come over here—hunt sheep. What for you settum trap?"

"Settum trap—ketch you," answered Wunpost succinctly. "You bad Injun—maybeso I kill you. Who hired you to come over here and kill me?"

Again the sullen silence, the stubborn turn of the head, the suffering compression of the lips; and Wunpost went back to his camp. The Indian was an Apache, he had known it from the start by his *tewas* and the cut of his hair; for no Indian in California wears high-topped buckskin moccasins with a little canoe-prow on the toe.

229

That was a mountain-Apache device, that little disc of rawhide, to protect the wearer's toes from rocks and cactus, and someone had imported this buck. Of course, it was Lynch but it was different to make him *say* so—but Wunpost knew how an Apache would go about it. He would light a little fire under his fellow-man and see if that wouldn't help. However there are ways which answer just as well, and Wunpost packed and mounted and rode down past the trap. Or at least he tried to, but his mules were so frightened that it took all his strength to haze them past. As for Good Luck, he flew at the Indian in a fury of barking and was nearly struck dead by a rock. The Apache was fighting mad, until Wunpost came back and tamed him; and then Wunpost spoke straight out.

"Here, you!" he said, "you savvy coyote? You want him come eat you up? Well, *talk* then, you dastard; or I'll go off and leave you. Come through now—who brought you over here?"

The Apache looked up at him from under his banged hair and his evil eyes roved fearfully about.

"Big fat man," he lied and Wunpost smiled grimly—he would tell this later to Eells.

"Nope," he said and shook his head warningly at which the Indian seemed to meditate his plight.

"Big tall man," he amended and Wunpost nodded.

"Sure," he said. "What name you callum?"

"Callum Lynchie," admitted the Apache with a sickly grin, "she come San Carlos—*busca* scout."

"Oh, *busca* scout, eh?" repeated Wunpost. "What for wantum scout? Plenty Shooshonnie scout, over here."

"Hah! Shooshonnie no good!" spat the Apache contemptuously. "Me *scout*—me work for Government! Injun scout—you savvy? Follow tracks for soldier. Me Manuel Apache—big chief!"

"Yes, big chief!" scoffed Wunpost, "but you ain't no scout, Manuel, or you wouldn't be caught here in this trap. Now listen, Mr. Injun— you want to go home? You want to go see your squaw? Well, s'pose I let you loose, what you think you're going to do—follow me up and shoot me for Lynch?"

"No! No shootum for Lynchie!" denied the Apache vigorously. "Lynchie—she say, *busca* mine! *Busca* gol' mine, savvy—but 'nother man she say, you ketchum plenty money—in pants."

"O-ho!" exclaimed Wunpost as the idea suddenly dawned on him and once more he experienced a twinge of regret. This time it was for the occasion when he had shown scornful Blackwater that seven thousand dollars in bills. And he had with him now—in his pants, as the Indian said—no less than thirty thousand dollars

231

in one roll. And all because he had lost his faith in banks.

"You shoot me—get money?" he inquired, slapping his leg; and Manuel Apache grinned guiltily. He was caught now, and ashamed, but not of attempting murder—he was ashamed of having been caught.

"Trap hurt!" he complained, drawing up his wrinkled face and rattling his chain impatiently, and Wunpost nodded gravely.

"All right," he said, "I'll turn you loose. A man that will flash his roll like I did in Blackwater—he *deserves* to get shot in the leg."

He took his rope from the saddle and noosed the Indian about both arms, after which he stretched him out as he would a fighting wildcat and loosened the springs with his clamps.

"What you do?" he inquired, "if I let you go?"

"Go home!" snarled Manuel, "Lynchie no good—me no likum. Me your friend—no shootum—go home!"

"Well, you'd better," warned Wunpost, "because next time I'll kill you. Oh, by grab, I nearly forgot!"

He whipped out the butcher-knife which the Apache had flung at him and cropped off a lock of his hair. It was something he had promised Wilhelmina.

232

CHAPTER XXII

THE FEAR OF THE HILLS

WUNPOST romped off down the canyon, holding the hair up like a scalp-lock—which it was, except for the scalp. Manuel Apache, with the pride of his kind, had knotted it up in a purple silk handkerchief; and he had yelled louder when he found it was gone than he had when he was caught in the trap. He had, in fact, acted extremely unreasonable, considering all that had been done for him; and Wunpost had been obliged to throw down on him with his six-shooter and order him off up the canyon. It was taking a big chance to allow him to live at all and, not to tempt him too far along the lines of reprisal, Wunpost left the Apache afoot. His gaunted pony was feeding hobbled, down the canyon, and Wunpost took off the rawhide thongs and hung them about his neck, after which he drove him on with his mules. But even at that he was taking a chance, or so at least it seemed, for the look in the Apache's eye as he had limped off up the gulch reminded Wunpost of a broken-backed rattlesnake.

He was a bad Indian and a bad actor—one of these men that throw butcher-knives—and yet Wunpost had tamed him and set him afoot and come off with his back hair, as promised. He was a Government scout, the pick of the Apaches, and he had matched his desert craft against Wunpost's; but that craft, while it was good, was not good enough, and he had walked right into a bear-trap. Not the trap in the trail—he had gone around that—but the one in the rocks, with the step-diverting bush pulled down. Wunpost had gauged it to a nicety and this big chief of the Apaches had lost out in the duel of wits. He had lost his horse and he had lost his hair; and that pain in his heel would be a warning for some time not to follow after Wunpost, the desert-man.

There were others, of course, who claimed to be desert-men and to know Death Valley like a book; but it was self-evident to Wunpost as he rode back with his trophies that he was the king of them all. He had taken on Lynch and his desert-bred Shoshone and led them the devil's own chase; and now he had taken on Manuel, the big chief of the Apaches, and left him afoot in the rocks. But one thing he had learned from this snakey-eyed man-killer—he would better get rid of his money. For there were others still in the hills who might pot him for it any time—and besides, it was a useless risk. He was taking chances enough without making it an object for every miscreant in the country to shoot him.

He camped that noon at Surveyor's Well, to give his mules a good feed of grass, and as he sat out in the open the two ravens came by, but now he laughed at their croaks. Even if the eagles came by he would not lose his nerve again, for he was fighting against men that he knew. Pisenface Lynch and his gang were no better than he was—they left a track and followed the trails—and after he had announced that his money was all banked they would have no inducement to kill him. The inducements, in fact, would be all the other way; because the man that killed him would be fully as foolish as the one that killed the goose for her egg. He alone was the repository of that great and golden secret, the whereabouts of the Sockdolager Mine; and if they killed him out of spite neither Eells nor any of his man-hunters would ever see the color of its ore.

Wunpost stretched his arms and laughed, but as he was saddling up his mules he saw a smoke, rising up from the mouth of Tank Canyon. It was not in the Canyon but high up on a point and he knew it was Manuel Apache. He was signaling across the Valley to his boss in the Panamints that he was in distress and needed help, but no answering smoke rose up from Tucki Mountain to show where Wunpost's enemies lay hid. The Panamints stood out clean in the brilliant November light and each purple canyon seemed to invite him to its shelter, so sweetly did they lie in the sun. And yet, as that thin smoke bellied up

235

and was smothered back again in the smoke-talk that the Apaches know so well, Wunpost wondered if its message was only a call for help—it might be a warning to Lynch. Or it might be a signal to still other Apaches who were watching his coming from the heights, and as Wunpost looked again his hand sought out the Indian's scalp-lock and he regarded it almost regretfully.

Why had he envenomed that ruthless savage by lifting his scalp-lock, the token of his warrior's pride; when by treating him generously he might have won his good will and thus have one less enemy in the hills? Perhaps Wilhelmina had been right—it was to make good on a boast which might much better have never been uttered. He had bet her his mine and everything he had, a thing quite unnecessary to do; and then to make good he had deprived this Indian of his hair, which alone might put him back on his trail. He might get another horse and take up once more that relentless and murderous pursuit; and this time, like Lynch, he would be out for blood and not for the money there was in it.

Wunpost sighed and cinched his packs and hit out across the flats for the mouth of Emigrant Wash. But the thought that other Apaches might be in Lynch's employ quite poisoned Wunpost's flowing cup of happiness, and as he drew near the gap which led off to Emigrant Springs he stopped and looked up at the mountains. They were high, he knew, and his mules were tired, but something told him not to go through that gap. It was a narrow passageway through the hills, not forty feet wide, and all along its sides there were caves in the cliffs where a hundred men could hide. And why should Manuel Apache be making fancy smoke-talks if no one but white men were there? Why not make a straight smoke, the way a white man would, and let it go at that? Wunpost shook his head sagely and turned away from the gap—he had had enough excitement for that trip.

Bone Canyon, for which he headed, was still far away and the sun was getting low; but Wunpost knew, even if others did not, that there was a water-hole well up towards the summit. A cloudburst had sluiced the canyon from top to bottom and spread out a great fan of dirt; but in the earlier days an Indian trail had wound up it, passing by the hidden spring. And if he could water his mules there he could rim out up above and camp on a broad, level flat. Wunpost jogged along fast, for he had left the pony at Surveyor's Well, and as he rode towards the canyon-mouth he kept his eyes on the ridges to guard against a possible surprise. For if Lynch and his Indians were watching from the gap they would notice his turning off to the left, and in that case a good runner might cut across to Bone Canyon before he could get through the pass. But the mountain side was empty and as the dusk was gathering he passed through the portals of Bone Canyon.

Like all desert canyons it boxed in at its mouth, opening out later in a broad valley behind; his road was the sand-wash, the path of the last cloudburst, now packed hard and set like stone. In the middle of the sand-wash a little channel had been dug by the last of the sluicing water; above the wash there rose another cut-bank where the cloudburst before it had taken out an even greater slice; and then on both sides there rose high bluffs of conglomerate which some father of all the cloudbursts had formed. Wunpost was riding in the lead now on his fast-walking mule, the two pack-animals following wearily along behind; in his nest on the front pack Good Luck was more than half sleeping, Wunpost himself was tempted to nod—and then, from the west bluff, there was a spit of fire and Wunpost found himself on the ground.

Across his breast and under his arm there was a streak that burned like fire, his mules were milling and bashing their packs; and as they turned both ways and ran he rolled over into the channel, with his rifle still clutched in one hand. Those days of steady practise had not been in vain, for as he went off his mule he had snatched at his saddle-gun and dragged it from its scabbard. And now he lay and waited, listening to the running of his mules and the frenzied barking of his dog; and it came to him vaguely that several shots had been fired, and some from the east bank of the wash. But the man who had hit him had fired from the west and Wunpost crept down the wash and looked up.

A trickle of blood was running down his left arm from the bullet wound which had just missed his heart, but his whole body was tingling with a strength which could move mountains and he was consumed with a passion for revenge. For the second time he had been ambushed and shot by this gang of cold-blooded murderers, and he had no doubt that their motive was the same as that to which the Indian had confessed. They had dogged his steps to kill him for his money—Pisen-face Lynch, or whoever it was—but their shooting was poor and as he rose beside a bush Wunpost took a chance from the east. The man he was looking for had shot from the west and he ran his eyes along the bluff.

Nothing stirred for a minute and then a round rock suddenly moved and altered its shape. He thrust out his rifle and drew down on it carefully, but the dusk put a blur on his sights. His foresight was beginning to loom, his hindsight was not clean, and he knew that would make him shoot high. He waited, all a-tremble, the sweat running off his face and mingling with the blood from his arm; and then the man rose up, head and shoulders against the sky, and he knew his

239

would-be murderer was Lynch. Wunpost held his gun against the light until the sights were lined up fine, then swung back for a snap-shot at Lynch; and as the rifle belched and kicked he caught a flash of a tumbling form and clutching hands thrown up wildly against the sky. Then he stooped down and ran, helter-skelter down the wash, regardless of what might be in his way; and as he plunged around a curve he stampeded a pack-mule which had run that far and stopped.

It was the smallest of his mules, and the wildest as well, Old Walker and his mate having gone off up the canyon in a panic which would take them to the ranch; but it was a mule and, being packed, it could not run far down hill so Wunpost walked up on it and caught it. Far out in the open, where no enemy could slip up on him, he halted and made a saddle of the pack, and as he mounted to go he turned to Tucki Mountain and called down a curse on Lynch. Then he rode back down the trail that led to Death Valley, for the fear of the hills had come back.

CHAPTER XXIII

THE RETURN OF THE BLOW-HARD

NOTHING was seen of John C. Calhoun for nearly a week and then, late one evening, he stepped in on Judson Eells in his office at the Blackwater Bank.

"Why—why, Mr. Calhoun!" he gasped, "we—we all thought you were dead!"

"Yes," returned Calhoun, whose arm was in a sling, "I thought so myself for a while. What's the good word from Mr. Lynch?"

Eells dropped back in his chair and stared at him fixedly.

"Why—we haven't been able to locate him. But you, Mr. Calhoun—we've been looking for you everywhere. Your riding mule came back with his saddle all bloody and a bullet wound across his hip and the Campbells were terribly distressed. We've had search-parties out everywhere but no one could find you and at last you were given up for dead."

"Yes, I saw some of those search-parties" answered Wunpost grimly, "but I noticed that they all packed Winchesters. What's the idee in trying to kill me?"

"Why, we aren't trying to kill you!" burst out Judson Eells vehemently. "Quite the contrary,

241

we've been trying to find you. But perhaps you can tell us about poor Mr. Lynch—he has disappeared completely."

"What about them Apaches?" inquired Wunpost pointedly, and Judson Eells went white.

"Why—what Apaches?" he faltered at last and Wunpost regarded him sternly.

"All right," he said, "I don't know nothing if you don't. But I reckon they turned the trick. That Manuel Apache was a bad one." He reached back into his hip-pocket and drew out a coiled-up scalp-lock. "There's his hair," he stated, and smiled.

"What? Did you kill him?" cried Eells, starting up from his chair, but Wunpost only shrugged enigmatically.

"I ain't talking," he said. "Done too much of that already. What I've come to say is that I've buried all my money and I'm not going back to that mine. So you can call off your bad-men and your murdering Apache Indians, because there's no use following me now. Thinking about taking a little trip for my health."

He paused expectantly but Judson Eells was too shocked to make any proper response. His world was tumbling about him, all his plans had come to naught—and Lynch was gone. He longed to question further, to seek out some clew, but he dared not, for his hands were not clean. He had hired this Apache whose grisly scalp-lock now lay before him, and the others who had been with Lynch; and if it ever became known— He shuddered and let his lip drop.

"This is horrible!" he burst out hoarsely, "but why should they kill Lynch?"

"And why should they kill *me?*" added Wunpost. "You've got a nerve," he went on, "bringing those devils into the country—don't you know they're as treacherous as a rattle-snake? No, you've been going too far; and it's a question with me whether I won't report the whole business to the sheriff. But what's the use of making trouble? All I want is that contract—and this time I reckon I'll get it."

He nodded confidently but Judson Eells' proud lip went up and instantly he became the bold financier.

"No," he said, "you'll never get it, Mr. Calhoun—not until you take me to the Sockdolager Mine."

"Nothing doing," replied Wunpost, "not for you or any other man. I stay away from that mine, from now on. Why should I give up a half—ain't I got thirty thousand dollars, hid out up here under a stone? Live and let live, sez I, and if you'll call off your bad-men I'll agree not to talk to the sheriff."

"You can talk all you wish!" snapped out Eells with rising courage, "I'm not afraid of your threats. And neither am I afraid of anything you can do to test the validity of that contract. It will hold, absolutely, in any court in the land; but if you will take me to your mine and turn it over in good faith, I will agree to cancel the contract."

"Oh! You don't want nothing!" hooted Wunpost sarcastically, "but I'll tell you what I will do—I'll give you thirty thousand dollars, cash."

"No! I've told you my terms, and there's no use coming back to me—it's the Sockdolager Mine or nothing."

"Suit yourself," returned Wunpost, "but I'm just beginning to wonder whether I'm shooting it out with the right men. What's the use of fighting murderers, and playing tag with Apache Indians, when the man that sends 'em out is sitting tight? In fact, why don't I come in here and get *you?*"

"Because you're wrong!" answered Eells without giving back an inch, "you're trying to evade the law. And any man that breaks the law is a coward at heart, because he knows that all society is against him."

"Sounds good," admitted Wunpost, "and I'd almost believe it if *you* didn't show such a nerve. But you know and I know that you break the law every day—and some time, Mr. Banker, you're going to get caught. No, you can guess again on why I don't shoot you—I just like to see you wiggle. I just like to see a big fat slob like you, that's got the whole world bluffed, twist around

244

in his seat when a *man* comes along and tells him what a dastard he is. And besides, I git a laugh, every time I come back and you make me think of the Stinging Lizard—and the road! But the biggest laugh I get is when you pull this virtuous stuff, like the widow-robbing old screw you are, and then have the nerve to tell me to my face that it's the Sockdolager Mine or nothing. Well, it's nothing then, Mr. Penny-pincher; and if I ever get the chance I'll make you squeal like a pig. And don't send no more Apaches after *me!*"

He rose up and slapped the desk, then picked up the scalp-lock and strode majestically out the door. But Judson Eells was unimpressed, for he had seen them squirm before. He was a banker, and he knew all the signs. Nor did John C. Calhoun laugh as he rode off through the night, for his schemes had gone awry again. Every word that he had said was as true as Gospel and he could sit around and wait a life-time—but waiting was not his long suit. In Los Angeles he seemed to attract all the bar-flies in the city, who swarmed about and bummed him for the drinks; and no man could stand their company for more than a few days without getting thoroughly disgusted. And on the desert, every time he went out into the hills he was lucky to come back with his life. So what was he to do, while he was waiting around for this banker to find out he was whipped?

245

For Eells was whipped, he was foiled at every turn; and yet that muley-cow lip came up as stubbornly as ever and he tried to tell him, Wunpost, he was wrong. And that because he was wrong and a law-breaker at heart he was therefore a coward and doomed to lose. It was ludicrous, the way Eells stood up for his "rights," when everyone knew he was a thief; and yet that purse-proud intolerance which is the hall-mark of his class made him think he was entirely right. He even had the nerve to preach little homilies about trying to evade the law. But that was it, his very self-sufficiency made him immune against anything but a club. He had got the idea into his George the Third head that the king can do no wrong—and he, of course was the king. If Wunpost made a threat, or concealed the location of a mine, that was wrong, it was against the law; but Eells himself had hired some assassins who had shot him, Wunpost, twice, and yet Eells was game to let it go before the sheriff—he could not believe he was wrong.

Wunpost cursed that pride of class which makes all capitalists so hard to head and put the whole matter from his mind. He had hoped to come back with that contract in his pocket, to show to the doubting Wilhelmina; but she had had enough of boasting and if he was ever to win her heart he must learn to feign a virtue which he lacked. That virtue was humility, the attribute of slaves and those who are not born to rule; but with her it was a virtue second only to that Scotch honesty which made upright Cole Campbell lean backwards. He was so straight he was crooked and cheated himself, so honest that he stood in his own light; and to carry out his principles he doomed his family to Jail Canyon for the rest of their natural lives. And yet Wilhelmina loved him and was always telling what he said and bragging of what he had done, when anyone could see that he was bull-headed as a mule and hadn't one chance in ten thousand to win. But all the same they were good folks, you always knew where you would find them, and Wilhelmina was as pretty as a picture.

No rouge on those cheeks and yet they were as pink as the petals of a blushing rose, and her lips were as red as Los Angeles cherries and her eyes were as honest as the day. Nothing fly about her, she had not learned the tricks that the candy-girls and waitresses knew, and yet she was as wise as many a grown man and could think circles around him when it came to an argument. She could see right through his bluffing and put her finger on the spot which convinced even him that he was wrong, but if he refrained from opposing her she was as simple as a child and her only desire was to please. She was not self-seeking, all she wanted was his company and a chance to give expression to her thoughts; and when he would listen they got on well enough, it was only when he boasted that she rebelled. For she could not endure his masculine complacency and his assumption that success made him right, and when he had gone away she had told him to his face that he was a blow-hard and his money was tainted.

Wunpost mulled this over, too, as he rode on up Jail Canyon and when he sighted the house he took Manuel Apache's scalp-lock and hid it inside his pack. After risking his life to bring his love this token he thought better of it and brought only himself. He would come back a friend, one who had seen trouble as they had but was not boasting of what he had done—and if anyone asked him what he had done to Lynch he would pass it off with some joke. So he talked too much, did he? All right, he would show them; he would close his trap and say nothing; and in a week Wilhelmina would be following him around everywhere, just begging to know about his arm. But no, he would tell her it was just a sad accident, which no one regretted more than he did; and rather than seem to boast he would say in a general way that it would never happen again. And that would be the truth, because from what Eells had said he was satisfied the Apaches had buried Lynch.

But how, now, was he to approach this matter of the money which he was determined to advance for the road? That would call for diplomacy and he would have to stick around a while before Billy would listen to reason. But once she was won over the whole family would be converted; for she was the boss, after all. She wore the overalls at the Jail Canyon Ranch and in spite of her pretty ways she had a will of her own that would not be denied. And when she saw him come back, like a man from the dead—he paused and blinked his eyes. But what would *he* say— would he tell her what had happened? No, there he was again, right back where he had started from—the thing for him to do was to *keep still*. Say nothing about Lynch and catching Apaches in bear-traps, just look happy and listen to her talk.

It was morning and the sun had just touched the house which hung like driftwood against the side of the hill. The mud of the cloudburst had turned to hard pudding-stone, which resounded beneath his mule's feet. The orchard was half buried, the garden in ruins, the corral still smothered with muck; but as he rode up the new trail a streak of white quit the house and came bounding down to meet him. It was Wilhelmina, still dressed in women's clothes but quite forgetful of everything but her joy; and when he dismounted she threw both arms about his neck, and cried when he gave her a kiss.

CHAPTER XXIV

SOMETHING NEW

THERE are compensations for everything, even for being given up for dead, and as he was welcomed back to life by a sweet kiss from Wilhelmina, Wunpost was actually glad he had been shot. He was glad he was hungry, for now she would feed him; glad he was wounded, for she would be his nurse; and when Cole Campbell and his wife took him in and made much of him he lost his last bitterness against Lynch. In the first place, Lynch was dead, and not up on the ridge waiting to pot him for what money he had; and in the second place Lynch had shot right past his heart and yet had barely wounded him at all. But the sight of that crease across his breast and the punctured hole through his arm quite disarmed the Campbells and turned their former disapproval to a hovering admiration and solicitude.

If the hand of Divine Providence had loosed the waterspout down their canyon to punish him for his overweening pride, perhaps it had now saved him and turned the bullet aside to make him meet for repentance. It was something like that which lay in their minds as they installed him in their best front room, and when they found that his hardships had left him chastened and silent they even consented to accept payment for his horse-feed. If they did not, he declared, he would pack up forthwith and take his whole outfit to Blackwater; and the fact was the Campbells were so reduced by their misfortunes that they had run up a big bill at the store. Only occasional contributions from their miner sons in Nevada kept them from facing actual want, and Campbell was engaged in packing down his picked ore in order to make a small shipment. But if he figured his own time in he was not making day's wages and the future held out no hope.

Without a road the Homestake Mine was worthless, for it could never be profitably worked; but Cole Campbell was like Eells in one respect at least, and that was he never knew when he was whipped. A guarded suggestion had come from Judson Eells that he might still be persuaded to buy his mine, but Campbell would not even name a price; and now the store-keeper had sent him notice that he had discounted his bill at the bank. That was a polite way of saying that Eells had bought in the account, which constituted a lien against the mine; and the Campbells were vaguely worried lest Eells should try his well-known tactics and suddenly deprive them of their treasure. For the Homestake Mine, in Cole Campbell's eyes, was the greatest silver property in the West; and yet even in this emergency, which threatened daily to become desperate, he refused resolutely to accept tainted money. For not only was Wunpost's money placed under the ban, but so much had been said of Judson Eells and his sharp practices that his money was also barred.

This much Wunpost gathered on the first day of his home-coming, when, still dazed by his welcome, he yet had the sense to look happy and say almost nothing. He sat back in an easy chair with Wilhelmina at his side and the Campbells hovering benevolently in the distance, and to all attempts to draw him out he responded with a cryptic smile.

"Oh, we were so worried!" exclaimed Wilhelmina, looking up at him anxiously, "because there was blood all over the saddle; and when the trailers got to Wild Rose they found your pack-mule, and Good Luck with the rope still fast about his neck. But they just couldn't find you anywhere, and the tracks all disappeared; and when it became known that Mr. Lynch was missing—oh, *do* you think they killed him?"

"Search me," shrugged Wunpost. "I was too busy getting out of there to do any worrying about Lynch. But I'll tell you one thing, about those tracks disappearing—them Apaches must have smoothed 'em out, sure."

"Yes, but why should they kill *him?* Weren't they supposed to be working for him? That's what Mr. Eells gave us to understand. But wasn't it kind of him, when he heard you were missing, to send all those search-parties out? It must have cost him several hundred dollars. And it shows that even the men we like the least are capable of generous impulses. He told Father he wouldn't have it happen for anything—I mean, for you to come to any harm. All he wanted, he said, was the mine."

"Yes," nodded Wunpost, and she ran on unheeding as he drew down the corners of his mouth. But he could agree to that quite readily, for he knew from his own experience that all Eells wanted was the mine. It was only a question now of what move he would make next to bring about the consummation of that wish. For it was Eells' next move, since, according to Wunpost's reasoning, the magnate was already whipped. His plans for tracing Wunpost to the source of his wealth had ended in absolute disaster and the only other move he could possibly make would be along the line of compromise. Wunpost had told him flat that he would not go near his mine, no one else knew even its probable location; and yet, when he had gone to him and suggested some compromise, Eells had refused even to consider it. Therefore he must have other plans in view.

But all this was far away and almost academic to the lovelorn John C. Calhoun, and if Eells never approached him on the matter of the Sockdolager it would be soon enough for him. What he wanted was the privilege of helping Billy feed the chickens and throw down hay to his mules, and then to wander off up the trail to the tunnel that opened out on the sordid world below. There the restless money-grabbers were rushing to and fro in their fight for what treasures they knew, but one kiss from Wilhelmina meant more to him now than all the gold in the world. But her kisses, like gold, came when least expected and were denied when he had hoped for them most; and the spell he held over her seemed once more near to breaking, for on the third day he forgot himself and talked. No, it was not just talk—he boasted of his mine, and there for the first time they jarred.

"Well, I don't care," declared Wilhelmina, "if you have got a rich mine! That's no reason for saying that Father's is no good; because it is, if it only had a road."

Now here, if ever, was the golden opportunity for remaining silent and looking intelligent; but Wunpost forgot his early resolve and gave way to an ill-timed jest.

"Yes," he said, "that's like the gag the Texas land-boomer pulled off when he woke up and

254

found himself in hell. 'If it only had a little more rain and good society—'"

"Now you hush up!" she cried, her lips beginning to tremble. "I guess we've got enough trouble, without your making fun of it—"

"No. I'm not making fun of you!" protested Wunpost stoutly. "Haven't I offered to build you a road? Well, what's the use of fiddling around, packing silver ore down on burros, when you know from the start it won't pay? First thing you folks know Judson Eells will come down on you and grab the whole mine for nothing. Why not take some of my money that I've buried under a rock and put in that aerial tramway?"

"Because we don't want to!" answered Wilhelmina tearfully; "my father wants a *road*. And I don't think it's very kind of you, after all we have suffered, to speak as if we were *fools*. If it wasn't for that waterspout that washed away our road we'd be richer than you are, today!"

"Oh, I don't know!" drawled Wunpost; "you don't know how rich I am. I can take my mules and be back here in three days with ten thousand dollars worth of ore!"

"You cannot!" she contradicted, and Wunpost's eyes began to bulge—he was not used to this lovely woman and her ways.

"Well, I'll just bet you I can," he responded deliberately. "What'll you bet that I can't turn the trick?"

"I haven't got anything to bet," retorted Wilhelmina angrily, "but if I did have, and it was right, I'd bet every cent I had—you're always making big brags!"

"Yes, so you say," replied Wunpost evenly, "but I'll tell you what I'll do. I'll put up a mule-load of ore against another sweet kiss—like you give me when I first came in."

Wilhelmina bowed her head and blushed painfully beneath her curls and then she turned away.

"I don't sell kisses," she said, and when he saw she was offended he put aside his arrogant ways.

"No, I know, kid," he said, "you were just glad to see me—but why can't you be glad all the time? Ain't I the same man? Well, you ought to be glad then, if you see me coming back again."

"But somebody might kill you!" she answered quickly, "and then I'd be to blame."

"They're scared to try it!" he boasted. "I've got 'em bluffed out. They ain't a man left in the hills. And besides, I told Eells I wouldn't go near the mine until he came through and sold me that contract. They's nobody watching me now. And you can take the ore, if you should happen to win, and build your father a road."

She straightened up and gazed at him with her honest brown eyes, and at last the look in them changed.

"Well, *I* don't care," she burst out recklessly, "and besides, you're not going to win."

"Yes I am," he said, "and I want that kiss, too. Here, pup!" and he whistled to his dog.

"Oh, you can't take Good Luck!" she objected quickly. "He's my dog now, and I want him!"

She pouted and tossed her pretty head to one side, and Wunpost smiled at her tyranny. It was something new in their relations with each other and it struck him as quite piquant and charming.

"Well, all right," he assented, and Billy hid her face; because treachery was new to her too.

CHAPTER XXV

THE CHALLENGE

IF love begets love and deceit begets deceit, then Wunpost was repaid according to his merits when Wilhelmina laid claim to his dog. She did it in a way that was almost coquettish, for coquetry is a form of deceit; but in the morning, when he was gone, she put his dog on his trail and followed along behind on her mule. And this, of course, was rank treachery no less, for her purpose was to discover his mine. If she found it, she had decided in the small hours of the night, she would locate it and claim it all; and that would teach him not to make fun of honest poverty or to try to buy kisses with gold. Because kisses, as she knew, could never be true unless they were given for love; and love itself calls for respect, first of all—and who can respect a boaster?

She reasoned in circles, as the best of us will when trying to justify doubtful acts; but she traveled in a straight line when she picked up Wunpost's trail and followed him over the rocks. He had ridden out in the night, turning straight up the ridge where the mountain-sheep trail came down; and Good Luck bounded ahead of her, his nose to the ground, his bobbed tail working like mad. There was a dew on the ground, for the nights had turned cold and, though he was no hound, Good Luck could follow the scent, which was only a few hours old. Wunpost had slept till after midnight and then silently departed, taking only Old Walker and his mate; and the trail of their sharp-shod shoes was easily discernible except where they went over smooth rocks. It was here that Wunpost circled, to throw off possible pursuit; but busy little Good Luck was frantic to come up to him, and he smelled out the tracks and led on.

Wunpost had traveled in the night, and, after circling a few times, his trail straightened out and fell into a dim path which had been traversed by mules once before. Up and up it led, until Tellurium was exhausted and Wilhelmina had to get off and walk; and at last, when it was almost at the summit of the range, it entered a great stone-patch and was lost. But the stone-patch was not limitless, and Wilhelmina was determined—she rode out around it, and soon Good Luck dropped his nose and set out straight to the south. To the south! That would take him into the canyon above Blackwater, where the pocket-miners had their claims; but surely the great Sockdolager was not over there, for the district had been worked for years.

Wilhelmina's heart stopped as she looked out the country from the high ridge beyond the stone-patch—could it be that his mine was close? Was it possible that his great strike was right there at their door while they had been searching for it clear across Death Valley? It was like the crafty Wunpost always to head north when his mine was hidden safely to the south; and yet how had it escaped the eyes of the prospectors who had been combing the hills for months? Where was it possible for a mine to be hid in all that expanse of peaks? She sat down on the summit and considered.

Happy Canyon lay below her, leading off to the west towards Blackwater and the Sink, and beyond and to the south there was a jumble of sharp-peaked hills painted with stripes of red and yellow and white. It was a rough country, and bone dry; perhaps the prospectors had avoided it and so failed to find his lost mine. Or perhaps he was throwing a circle out through this broken ground to come back by Hungry Bill's ranch. Wilhelmina sat and meditated, searching the country with the very glasses which Wunpost himself had given her; and Good Luck came back and whined. He had found his master's trail, it led on to the south, and now Wilhelmina would not come. She did not even take notice of him, and after watching her face Good Luck turned and ran resolutely on. He knew whose dog he was, even if she did not; and after calling to him perfunctorily Wilhelmina let him go, for even this defection might be used.

Wunpost was so puffed up with pride over the devotion of his dog that he would be pleased beyond measure to have him follow, and from her lookout on the ridge she could watch where Good Luck went and spy out the trail for miles. It was time to turn back if she was to reach home by dark, but that white, scurrying form was too good a marker and she followed him through her glasses for an hour. He would go bounding up some ridge and plunge down into the next canyon; and then, still running, he would top another summit until at last he was lost in a black canyon. It was different from the rest, its huge flank veiled in shadow until it was black as the entrance to a cavern; and the piebald point that crowned its southern rim was touched with a broad splash of white. Wilhelmina marked it well and then she turned back with crazy schemes still chasing through her brain.

Time and again Wunpost had boasted that his mine was not staked, and that it lay there a prize for the first man who found it or trailed him to his mine. Well, she, Wilhelmina, had trailed him part way; and after he was gone she would ride to that black canyon and look for big chunks of gold. And if she ever found his mine she would locate it for herself, and have her claim recorded; and then perhaps he would change his ways and stop calling her Billy and Kid. She was not a boy, and she was not a kid; but a grown-up woman, just as good as he was and, it might be, just as smart. And oh, if she could only find that hidden mine and dig out a mule-load of gold! It would serve him right, when he came back from Los Angeles or from having a good time inside, to find that his mine had been jumped by a girl and that she had taken him at his word. He had challenged her to find it, and dared her to stake it—very well, she would show him what a desert girl can do, once she makes up her mind to play the game.

He was always exhorting her to play the game, and to forget all that righteousness stuff—as if being righteous was worse than a crime, and a reflection upon the intelligence as well. But she would let him know that even the righteous can play the game, and if she could ever stake his mine she would show him no mercy until he confessed that he had been wrong. And then she would compel him to make his peace with Eells and—but that could be settled later. She rode home in a whirl, now imagining herself triumphant and laying down the law to him and Eells; then coming back to earth and thinking up excuses to offer when her lover returned. He might find her tracks, where she had followed on his trail—well, she would tell him about Good Luck, and how he had led her up the trail until at last he had run away and left her. And if he demanded the kiss—instead of asking for it nicely—well, that would be a good time to quarrel.

It was almost Machiavellian, the way she schemed and plotted, and upon her return home she burst into tears and informed her mother that Good Luck was lost. But her early training in the verities now stood her in good stead, for Good Luck *was* lost; so of course she was telling the truth, though it was a long way from being the whole truth. And the tears were real tears, for her conscience began to trouble her the moment she faced her mother. Yet as beginners at poker often win through their ignorance, and because nobody can tell when they will bluff, so Wilhelmina succeeded beyond measure in her first bout at "playing the game." For if her efforts lacked finesse she had a life-time of truth-telling to back up the clumsiest deceit. And besides, the Campbells had troubles of their own without picking at flaws in their daughter. She had come to an age when she was restive of all restraint and they wisely left her alone.

The second day of Wunpost's absence she went up to her father's mine and brought back the burros, packed with ore; but on the third day she stayed at home, working feverishly in her new garden and watching for Wunpost's return. His arm was not yet healed and he might injure it by digging, or his mules might fly back and hurt him; and ever since his departure she had thought of nothing else but those Apaches who had twice tried to murder him. What if they had spied him from the heights and followed him to his mine, or waylaid him and killed him for his money? She had not thought of that when she had made their foolish bet, but it left her sick with regrets. And if anything happened to him she could never forgive herself, for she would be the cause of it all. She watched the ridge till evening, then ran up to her lookout—and there he was, riding in from the *north*. Her heart stood still, for who would look for him there; and then as he waved at her she gathered up her hindering skirts and ran down the hill to meet him.

He rode in majestically, swaying about on his big mule; and behind him followed his pack-mule, weighed down with two kyacks of ore, and Good Luck was tied on the pack. Nothing had happened to him, he was safe—and yet something must have happened, for he was riding in from the north.

"Oh, I'm so glad!" she panted as he dropped down to greet her, and before she knew it she had rushed into his arms and given him the kiss and more. "I was afraid the Indians had killed you," she explained, and he patted her hands and stood dumb. Something poignant was striving within him for expression, but he could only pat her hands.

264

"Nope," he said and slipped his arm around her waist, at which Wilhelmina looked up and smiled. She had intended to quarrel with him, so he would depart for Los Angeles and leave her free to go steal his mine—but that was aeons ago, before she knew her own heart or realized how wrong it would be.

"You like me; don't you, kid?" he remarked at last, and she nodded and looked away.

"Sometimes," she admitted, "and then you spoil it all. You must take your arm away now."

He took his arm away, and then it crept back again in a rapturous, bear-like hug.

"Aw, quit your fooling, kid," he murmured in her ear, "you know you like me a lot. And say, I'm going to ask you a leading question—will you promise to answer 'Yes'?"

He laughed and let her go, all but one hand that he held, and then he drew her back.

"You know what I mean," he said. "I want you to be my wife."

He waited, but there was no answer; only a swaying away from him and a reluctant striving against his grip. "Come on," he urged, "let's go in to Los Angeles and you can help me spend my money. I've got lots of it, kid, and it's yours for the asking—the whole or any part of it. But you're too pretty a girl to be shut up here in Jail Canyon, working your hands off at packing ore and slaving around like Hungry Bill's daughters—"

"What do you mean?" she demanded, striking his hands aside and turning to face him angrily, and Wunpost saw he had gone too far.

"Aw, now, Wilhelmina," he pleaded, then fell into a sulky silence as she tossed back her curls and spoke.

"Don't you think," she burst out, "that I like to work for my father? Well, I do; and I ought to do more! And I'd like to know where Hungry Bill comes in—"

"He don't!" stated Wunpost, who was beginning to see red; but she rushed on, undeterred.

"—because you don't need to think I'm a *squaw*. We may be poor, but you can't buy *me*—and my father doesn't need to keep *watch* of me. I guess I've been brought up to act like a lady, if I did—oh, I just hate the sight of you!"

She ended a little weakly, for the memory of that kiss made her blush and hang her head; but Wunpost had been trained to match hate with a hate, and he reared up his mane and stepped back.

"Aw, who said you were a squaw?" he retorted arrogantly. "But you might as well be, by grab! Only old Hungry Bill takes his girls down to town, but you never git to go nowhere."

"I don't want to go!" she cried in a passion. "I

want to stay here and help all I can. But all you talk about now is how much money you've got, as if nothing else in the world ever counts."

"Well, forget it!" grumbled Wunpost, swinging up on his mule and starting off up the canyon. "I'll go off and give you a rest. And maybe them girls in Los Angeles won't treat me quite so high-headed."

"I don't care," began Wilhelmina—but she did, and so she stopped. And then the old plan, conceived aeons ago, rose up and took possession of her mind. She followed along behind him, and already in her thoughts she was the owner of the Sockdolager Mine. She held it for herself, without recognizing his claims or any that Eells might bring; and while she dug out the gold and shoveled it into sacks they stood by and looked on enviously. But when her mules were loaded she took the gold away and gave it to her father for his road.

"I don't care!" she repeated, and she meant it.

CHAPTER XXVI

THE FINE PRINT

A WEEK passed by, and Wilhelmina rode into Blackwater and mailed a letter to the County Recorder; and a week later she came back, to receive a letter in return and to buy at the store with gold. And then the big news broke—the Sockdolager had been found—and there was a stampede that went clear to the peaks. Blackwater was abandoned, and swarming again the next day with the second wave of stampeders; and the day after that John C. Calhoun piled out of the stage and demanded to see Wilhelmina. He hardly knew her at first, for she had bought a new dress; and she sat in an office up over the bank, talking business with several important persons.

"What's this I hear?" he demanded truculently, when he had cleared the room of all callers. "I hear you've located my mine."

"Yes, I have," she admitted. "But of course it wasn't yours—and besides, you said I could have it."

"Where is it at?" he snapped, sweating and fighting back his hair, and when she told him he groaned.

"How'd you find it?" he asked, and then he

groaned again, for she had followed his own fresh trail.

"Stung!" he moaned and sank down in a chair, at which she dimpled prettily.

"Yes," she said, "but it was all for your own good. And anyway, you dared me to do it."

"Yes, I did," he assented with a weary sigh. "Well, what do you want me to do?"

"Why, nothing," she returned. "I'm going to sell out to Mr. Eells and—"

"To Eells!" he yelled. "Well, by the holy, jumping Judas—how much is he going to give you?"

"Forty thousand dollars and—"

"*Forty thousand!* Say, she's worth forty *million!* For cripes' sake—have you signed the papers?"

"No, I haven't, but—"

"Well, then, *don't!* Don't you do it—don't you dare to sign anything, not even a receipt for your money! Oh, my Lord, I just got here in time!"

"But I'm going to," ended Wilhelmina, and then for the first time he noticed the look in her eye. It was as cold and steely as a gun-fighter's.

"Why—what's the matter?" he clamored. "You ain't sore at me, are you? But even if you are, don't sign any papers until I tell you about that mine. How much ore have you got in sight?"

"Why, just that one vein, where it goes under the black rock—"

"They's two others!" he panted, "that I covered up on purpose. Oh, my Lord, this is simply awful."

"Two others!" echoed Wilhelmina, and then she sat dumb while a scared look crept into her eyes. "Well, I didn't know that," she went on at last, "and of course we lost everything, that other time. So when Mr. Eells offered me forty thousand cash and agreed to release you from that grubstake contract—"

"You throwed the whole thing away, eh?"

He had turned sullen now and petulantly discontented and the fire flashed back into her eyes.

"Well, is that all the thanks I get? I thought you *wanted* that contract!"

"I did!" he complained, "but if you'd left me alone I'd 've got it away from him for nothing. But forty thousand dollars! Say, what's your doggoned hurry—have you got to sell out the first day?"

"No, but that time before, when he tried to buy us out I held on until I didn't get anything. And Father has been waiting for his road *so* long—"

"Oh, that road again!" snarled Wunpost. "Is that all you think about? You've thrown away millions of dollars!"

"Well, anyway, I've got the road!" she answered with spirit, "and that's more than I did before. If I'd followed my own judgment instead of taking your advice—"

"Your judgment!" he mocked; "say, shake yourself, kid—you've pulled the biggest bonehead of a life-time."

"I don't care!" she answered, "I'll get forty thousand dollars. And if Father builds his road our mine will be worth millions, so why shouldn't I let this one go?"

"Oh, boys!" sighed Wunpost and slumped down in his chair, then roused up with a wild look in his eyes. "You haven't signed up, have you?" he demanded again. "Well, thank God, then, I got here in time!"

"No you didn't," she said, "because I told him I'd do it and we've already drawn up the papers. At first he wouldn't hear to it, to release you from your contract; but when I told him I wouldn't sell without it, he and Lapham had a conference and they're downstairs now having it copied. There are to be three copies, one for each of us and one for you, because of course you're an interested party. And I thought, if you were released, you could go out and find another mine and—"

"Another one!" raved Wunpost. "Say, you must think it's easy! I'll never find another one in a life-time. Another Sockdolager? I could sell that mine tomorrow for a million dollars, cash; it's got a hundred thousand dollars in sight!"

"Well, that's what you told me when we had the Willie Meena, and now already they say it's worked out—and I know Mr. Eells isn't rich. He had to send to Los Angeles to get the money for this first payment—"

"What, have you accepted his *money?*" shouted Wunpost accusingly, and Wilhelmina rose to her feet.

"Mr. Calhoun," she said, "I'll have you to understand that I own this mine myself. And I'm not going to sit here and be yelled at like a Mexican—not by you or anybody else."

"Oh, it's yours, is it?" he jeered. "Well, excuse me for living; but who came across it in the first place?"

"Well, you did," she conceded, "and if you hadn't been always bragging about it you might be owning it yet. But you were always showing off, and making fun of my father, and saying we were all such *fools*—so I thought I'd just *show* you, and it's no use talking now, because I've agreed to sell it to Eells."

"That's all right, kid," he nodded, after a long minute of silence. "I reckon I had it coming to me. But, by grab, I never thought that little Billy Campbell would throw the hooks into me like this."

"No, and I wouldn't," she returned, "only you just treated us like dirt. I'm glad, and I'd do it again."

"Well, I've learned one thing," he muttered gloomily; "I'll never trust a woman again."

"Now isn't that just like a man!" exclaimed Wilhelmina indignantly. "You know you never trusted anybody. I asked you one time where you got all that ore and you looked smart and said: 'That's a question. If I'd tell you, you'd know the answer.' Those were the very words you said. And now you'll never trust a woman again!"

She laughed, and Wunpost rose slowly to his feet, but he did not get out of the door.

"What's the matter?" she taunted; "did 'them Los Angeles girls' fool you, too? Or am I the only one?"

"You're the only one," he answered ambiguously, and stood looking at her queerly.

"Well, cheer up!" she dimpled, for her mood was gay. "You'll find another one, somewhere."

"No I won't," he said; "you're the only one, Billy. But I never looked for nothing like this."

"Well, you told me to get onto myself and learn to play the game, and finally I took you at your word."

"Yes," he agreed, "I can't say a word. But these Blackwater stiffs will sure throw it into me when they find I've been trimmed by a girl. The best thing I can do is to drift."

He put his hand on the door-knob, but she knew he would not go, and he turned back with a sheepish grin.

"What do the folks think about this?" he inquired casually, and Wilhelmina made a face.

"They think I'm just *awful!*" she confessed. "But I don't care—I'm tired of being poor."

"Don't reckon there'll be another cloudburst, do you, about the time you get your road built?"

She grew sober at that and then her eyes gleamed.

"I don't care!" she repeated, "and besides, I didn't steal this. You told me I could have it, you know."

"Too fine a point for me," he decided. "We'll just see, after you build your new road."

"Well, I'm going to build it," she stated, "because he'll worry himself to death. And I don't care what happens to me, as long as he gets his road."

"Well, I've seen 'em that wanted all kinds of things, but you're the first one that wanted a road. And so you're going to sign this contract if it loses you a million dollars?"

"Yes, I am," she said. "We've drawn it all up and I've given him my word, so there's nothing else to do."

"Yes, there is," he replied. "Tell him you've changed your mind and want a million dollars. Tell him that I've come back and don't want that grubstake contract and that you'll take it all in cash."

"No," she frowned, "now there's no use

arguing, because I've fully made up my mind. And if—" She paused and listened as steps came down the hall. "They're coming," she said and smiled.

There was a rapid patter of feet and Lapham rapped and came in, bearing some papers and his notary's stamp; but when he saw Wunpost he stopped and stood aghast, while his stamp fell to the floor with a bang.

"Why, why—oh, excuse me!" he broke out, turning to dart through the door; but the mighty bulk of Eells had blocked his way and now it forced him back.

"Why—what's this?" demanded Eells, and then he saw Wunpost and his lip dropped down and came up. "Oh, excuse me, Miss Campbell," he burst out hastily, "we'll come back—didn't know you were occupied." He started to back out and Wunpost and Wilhelmina exchanged glances, for they had never seen him flustered before. But now he was stampeded, though why they could not guess, for he had never feared Wunpost before.

"Oh, don't go!" cried Wilhelmina; "we were just waiting for you to come. *Please* come back—I want to have it over with."

She flew to the door and held it open and Eells and his lawyer filed in.

"Don't let me disturb you," said Wunpost grimly and stood with his back to the wall. There

275

was something in the wind, he could guess that already, and he waited to see what would happen. But if Eells had been startled his nerve had returned, and he proceeded with ponderous dignity.

"This won't take but a moment," he observed to Wilhelmina as he spread the papers before her. "Here are the three copies of our agreement and"—he shook out his fountain pen—"you put your name right there."

"No you don't!" spoke up Wunpost, breaking in on the spell, "don't sign nothing that you haven't read."

He fixed her with his eyes and as Wilhelmina read his thoughts she laid down the waiting pen. Eells drew up his lip, Lapham shuffled uneasily, and Wilhelmina took up the contract. She glanced through it page by page, dipping in here and there and then turning impatiently ahead; and as she struggled with its verbiage the sweat burst from Eells' face and ran unnoticed down his neck.

"All right," she smiled, and was picking up the pen when she paused and turned hurriedly back.

"Anything the matter?" croaked Lapham, clearing his throat and hovering over her, and Wilhelmina looked up helplessly.

"Yes; please show me the place where it tells about that contract—the one for Mr. Calhoun."

"Oh—yes," stammered Lapham, and then he

hesitated and glanced across at Eells. "Why—er—" he began, running rapidly through the sheets, and John C. Calhoun strode forward.

"What did I tell you?" he said, nodding significantly at Wilhelmina and grabbing up the damning papers. "That'll do for you," he said to Lapham. "We'll have you in the Pen for this." And when Lapham and Eells both rushed at him at once he struck them aside with one hand. For they did not come on fighting, but all in a tremble, clutching wildly to get back the papers.

"I knowed it," announced Wunpost; "that clause isn't there. This is one time when we read the fine print."

CHAPTER XXVII

A COME-BACK

IT takes an iron nerve to come back for more punishment right after a solar plexus blow, but Judson Eells had that kind. Phillip F. Lapham went to pieces and began to beg, but Eells reached out for the papers.

"Just give me that contract," he suggested amiably; "there must be some mistake."

"Yes, you bet there's a mistake," came back Wunpost triumphantly, "but we'll show these papers to the judge. This ain't the first time you've tried to put one over, but you robbed us once before."

He turned to Wilhelmina, whose eyes were dark with rage, and she nodded and stood close beside him.

"Yes," she said, "and I was selling it for almost nothing, just to get that miserable grubstake. Oh, I think you just ought to be—hung!"

She took one of the contracts and ran through it to make sure, and Eells coughed and sent Lapham away.

"Now let's sit down," he said, "and talk this matter over. And if, through an oversight, the clause has been left out perhaps we can make other arrangements."

"Nothing doing," declared Wunpost. "You're a crook and you know it; and I don't want that grubstake contract, nohow. And there's a feller in town that I know for a certainty will give five hundred thousand dollars, cash."

"Oh, no!" protested Eells, but his glance was uneasy and he smiled when Wilhelmina spoke up.

"Well, I *do!*" she said. "I want that grubstake contract cancelled. But forty thousand dollars—"

"I'll give you more," put in Eells, suddenly coming to life. "I'll bond your mine for a hundred thousand dollars if you'll give me a little more time."

"And will you bring out that grubstake contract and have it cancelled in my presence?" demanded Wilhelmina peremptorily, and Eells bowed before the storm.

"Yes, I'll do that," he agreed, "although a hundred thousand dollars—"

"There's a hundred thousand in sight!" broke in Wunpost intolerantly. "But what do you want to trade with a crook like that for?" he demanded of Wilhelmina, "when I can get you a certified check? Is he the only man in town that can buy your mine? I'll bet you I can find you twenty. And if you don't get an offer of five hundred thousand cash—"

"I'll make it two hundred," interposed Judson

Eells hastily, "and surrender the cancelled grubstake!"

"I don't *want* the danged grubstake!" burst out Wunpost impatiently. "What good is it now, when my claim has been jumped and I ain't got a prospect in sight? No, it ain't worth a cent, now that the Sockdolager is located, and I don't want it counted for anything."

"But *I* want it," objected Wilhelmina, "and I'm willing to let it count. But if others will pay me more—"

"I'll bond your mine," began Judson Eells desperately, "for four hundred thousand dollars—"

"Don't you do it," came back Wunpost, "because under a bond and lease he can take possession of your property. And if he ever gits a-hold of it—"

"I'm talking to Miss Campbell," blustered Eells indignantly, but his guns were spiked again. Wilhelmina knew his record too well, for he had driven her from the Willie Meena, and yet she lingered on.

"Suppose," she said at last, "I should sell my mine elsewhere; how much would you take for that grubstake?"

"I wouldn't sell it at any price!" returned Judson Eells instantly. "I'm convinced that he has other claims."

"Well, then, how much will you give me in

cash for my mine and throw the grubstake in?"

"I'll give you four hundred thousand dollars in four yearly payments—"

"Don't you do it," butted in Wunpost, but Wilhelmina turned upon him and he read the decision in her eye.

"I'll take it," she said. "But this time the papers will be drawn up by a lawyer that I will hire. And I must say, Mr. Eells, I think the way you changed those papers—"

"It ought to put him in the Pen," observed Wunpost vindictively. "You're easy—and you're compounding a felony."

"Well, I don't know what that is," answered Wilhelmina recklessly, "but anyway, I'll get that grubstake."

"Well, I know one thing," stated Wunpost. "I'm going to keep these papers until he makes the last of those payments. Because if he don't dig that gold out inside of four years it won't be because he don't *try*."

"No, you give them to me," she demanded, pouting, and Wunpost handed them over. This was a new one on him—Wilhelmina turning pouty! But the big fight was over, and when Eells went away she dismissed John C. Calhoun and cried.

It takes time to draw up an ironclad contract that will hold a man as slippery as Eells, but two outside lawyers who had come in with the rush did their best to make it air-tight. And even after that Wunpost took it to Los Angeles to show a lawyer who was his *friend*. When it came back from the friend there was a proviso against everything, including death and acts of God. But Judson Eells signed it and made a first payment of twenty-five thousand dollars down, after which John C. Calhoun suddenly dropped out of sight before Wilhelmina could thank him. She heard of him later as being in Los Angeles, and then he came back through Blackwater; but before she could see him he was gone again, on some mysterious errand into the hills. Then she returned to the ranch and missed him again, for he went by without making a stop. A month had gone by before she met him on the street, and then she *knew* he was avoiding her.

"Why, good morning, Miss Campbell," he exclaimed, bowing gallantly; "how's the mine and every little thing? You're looking fine, there's nothing to it; but say, I've got to be going!"

He started to rush on, but Wilhelmina stopped him and looked him reproachfully in the eye.

"Where have you been all the time?" she chided. "I've got something I want to give you."

"Well, keep it," he said, "and I'll drop in and get it. See you later." And he started to go.

"No, wait!" she implored, tagging resolutely

after him, and Wunpost halted reluctantly. "Now I *know* you're mad at me," she charged; "that's the first time you ever called me Miss Campbell."

"Is that so?" he replied. "Well, it must have been the clothes. When you wore overalls you was Billy, and that white dress made it Wilhelmina; and now it's Miss Campbell, and then some."

He stopped and mopped the sweat from his perspiring brow, but he refused to meet her eye.

"Won't you come up to my office?" she asked very meekly. "I've got something important to tell you."

"Is that feller Eells trying to beat you out of your money?" he demanded with sudden heat, but she declined to discuss business on the street. In her office she sat him down and closed the door behind them, then drew out a contract from her desk.

"Here's that grubstake agreement, all cancelled," she said, and he took it and grunted ungraciously.

"All right," he rumbled; "now what's the important business? Is the bank going broke, or what?"

"Why, no," she answered, beginning to blink back the tears, "what makes you talk like that?"

"Well, I was just into Los Angeles, trying to round up that bank examiner, and I thought maybe he'd made his report."

"What—really?" she cried, "don't you think the bank is safe? Why, all my money is there!"

"How much you got?" he asked, and when she told him he snorted. "Twenty-five thousand, eh?" he said. "How'd he pay you—with a check? Well, he might not have had a cent. A man that will rob a girl will rob his depositors—you'd better draw out a few hundred."

She rose up in alarm, but something in his smile made her sit down and eye him accusingly.

"I know what you're doing," she said at last; "you're trying to break his bank. You always said you would."

"Oh, that stuff!" he jeered, "that was nothing but hot air. I'm a blow-hard—everybody knows that."

She looked at him again, and her face became very grave, for she knew what was gnawing at his heart. And she was far from being convinced.

"You didn't thank me," she said, "for returning your grubstake. Does that mean you really don't care? Or are you just mad because I took away your mine? Of course I know you are."

"Sure, I'm mad," he admitted. "Wouldn't you be mad? Well, why should I thank you for this? You take away my mine, that was worth millions of dollars, and gimme back a piece of paper."

He slapped the contract against his leg and thrust it roughly into his shirt, at which Wilhelmina burst into tears.

"I—I'm sorry I stole it," she confessed between sobs, "and now Father and everybody is against me. But I did it for you—so you wouldn't get killed—and so Father could have his road. And now he won't take it, because the money isn't ours. He says I'm to return it to you."

"Well, you tell your old man," burst out Wunpost brutally, "that he's crazy and I won't touch a cent. I guess I know how to get my rights without any help from him."

"Why, what do you mean?" she queried tremulously, but he shut his mouth down grimly.

"Never mind," he said, "you just hold your breath, and listen for something to drop. I ain't through, by no manner of means."

"Oh, you're going to fight Eells!" she cried out reproachfully. "I just know something dreadful will happen."

"You bet your life it will—but not to me. I'm after that old boy's hide."

"And won't you take the money?" she asked regretfully, and when he shook his head she wept. It was not easy weeping, for Wilhelmina was not the kind that practices before a mirror, and the agony of it touched his heart.

"Aw, say, kid," he protested, "don't take on like that—the world hasn't come to an end. You ain't cut out for this rough stuff, even if you did steal me blind, but I'm not so sore as all that. You tell your old man that I'll accept ten thousand dollars

285

if he'll let me rebuild that road—because ever since it washed out I've felt conscience-stricken as hell over starting that cloudburst down his canyon."

He rose up gaily, but she refused to be comforted until he laid his big hand on her head, and then she sprang up and threw both arms around his neck and made him give her a kiss. But she did not ask him to forgive her.

CHAPTER XXVIII

WUNPOST HAS A BAD DREAM

IT is dangerous to start rumors against even the soundest of banks, because our present-day finance is no more than a house of cards built precariously on Public Confidence. No bank can pay interest, or even do business, if it keeps all its money in the vaults; and yet in times of panic, if a run ever starts, every depositor comes clamoring for his money. Public confidence is shaken—and the house of cards falls, carrying with it the fortunes of all. The depositors lose their money, the bankers lose their money; and thousands of other people in nowise connected with it are ruined by the failure of one bank. Hence the committee of Blackwater citizens, with blood in their eye, which called on John C. Calhoun.

Since the loss of his mine Wunpost had turned ugly and morose; and his remarks about Eels, and especially about his bank, were nicely calculated to get under the rind. He was waiting for the committee, right in front of the bank; and the moment they began to talk he began to orate, and to denounce them and everything else in Blackwater. What was intended as a call-down of an envious and destructive agitator threatened momentarily to turn into a riot and, hearing his own good name brought into question, Judson Eells stepped quickly out and challenged his bold traducer.

"W'y, sure I said it!" answered Wunpost hotly, "and I don't mind saying it again. Your bank is all a fake, like your danged tin front; and you've got everything in your vault except money."

"Well, now, Mr. Calhoun," returned Judson Eells waspishly, "I'm going to challenge that statement, right now. What authority have you got for suggesting that my cash is less than the law requires?"

"Well," began Wunpost, "of course I don't *know,* but—"

"No, of course you don't know!" replied Eells with a smile, "and everybody knows you don't know; but your remarks are actionable and if you don't shut up and go away I'll instruct my attorney to sue you."

"Oh, 'shut up,' eh?" repeated Wunpost after the crowd had had its laugh; "you think I'm a blow-hard, eh? You all do, don't you? Well, I'll tell you what I'll do." He paused impressively, reached down into several pockets and pointed a finger at Eells. "I'll bet you," he said, "that I've got more money in my clothes than you have in your whole danged bank—and if you can prove any different I'll acknowledge I'm wrong by depositing my roll in your bank. Now—that's fair enough, ain't it?"

He nodded and leered knowingly at the gaping crowd as Eells began to temporize and hedge.

"I'm a blow-hard, am I?" he shouted uproariously; "my remarks are actionable, are they? Well, if I should go into court and tell half of what I know there'd be *two* men on their way to the Pen!" He pointed two fingers at Eells and Phillip Lapham and the banker saw a change in the crowd. Public confidence was wavering, the cold fingers of doubt were clutching at the hearts of his depositors—but behind it all he sensed a trap. It was not by accident that Wunpost was on his corner when the committee of citizens came by; and this bet of his was no accident either, but part of some carefully laid scheme. The question was—how much money did Wunpost have? If, unknown to them, he had found access to large sums and had come there with the money on his person, then the acceptance of his bet would simply result in a farce and make the bank a byword and a mocking. If it could be said on the street that one disreputable prospector had more money in his clothes than the bank, then public confidence would receive a shrewd blow indeed, which might lead to disastrous results. But the murmur of doubt was growing, Wunpost was ranting like a demagogue—the time for a show-down had come.

"Very well!" shouted Eells, and as the crowd began to cheer the committee adjourned to the bank. Eells strode in behind the counter and threw the vault doors open, his cashier and Lapham made the count, and when Wunpost was permitted to see the cash himself his face fell and he fumbled in his pockets.

"You win," he announced, and while all Blackwater whooped and capered he deposited his roll in the bank. It was a fabulously big roll—over forty thousand dollars in five hundred and thousand dollar bills—but he deposited it all without saying a word and went out to buy the drinks.

"That's all right," he said, "the drinks are on me. But I wanted to know that that money was *safe* before I went in and put it in the bank."

It was a great triumph for Eells and a great boost for his bank, and he insisted in the end upon shaking hands with Wunpost and assuring him there was no hard feeling. Wunpost took it all grimly, for he claimed to be a sport, but he saddled up soon after and departed for the hills, leaving Blackwater delirious with joy. So old Wunpost had been stung and called again by the redoubtable Judson Eells, and the bank had been proved to be perfectly sound and a credit to the community it served! It made pretty good reading for the *Blackwater Blade*, which had recently been established in their midst, and the committee of boosters ordered a thousand extra copies and sent them all over the country. That was real mining stuff, and every dollar of Wunpost's money had been dug from the Sockdolager Mine. Eells set to work immediately to build him a road and to order the supplies and machinery, and as the development work was pushed towards completion John C. Calhoun was almost forgotten. He was gone, that was all they knew, and if he never came back it would be soon enough for Eells.

But there was one who still watched for the prodigal's return and longed ardently for his coming, for Wilhelmina Campbell still remembered with regret the days when their ranch had been his goal. No matter where he had been, or what desperate errand took him once more into the hills, he had headed for their ranch like a homing pigeon that longs to join its mates. The portal of her tunnel had been their trysting place, where he had boasted and raged and denounced all his enemies and promised to return with their scalps. But that was just his way, and it was harmless after all, and wonderfully exciting and amusing; but now the ranch was dead, except for the gang of road-makers who came by from their camp up the canyon.

For her father at last had consented to build the road, since Wunpost had disclaimed all title to the mine; but now it was his daughter who looked on with a heavy heart, convinced that the money was accursed. She had stolen it, she knew, from the man who had been her lover and who had trusted her as no one else; only Wunpost was too proud to make any protest or even acknowledge he had been wronged. He had accepted his loss with the grim stoicism of a gambler and gone out again into the hills, and the only thought that rose up to comfort her was that he had deposited all his money in the bank. Every dollar, so they said; and when he had bought his supplies the store-keeper had had to write out his check! But anyway he was safe, for now everybody knew that he had no money on his person; and when he came back he might stop at the ranch and she could tell him about the road.

It was being built by contract, and more solidly than ever, and already it was through the gorge and well up the canyon towards Panamint and the Homestake Mine. And the mud and rocks that the cloudburst had deposited had been dug out and cleared away from their trees; the ditch had been enlarged, her garden restored and everything left tidy and clean. But something was lacking and, try as she would, she failed to feel the least thrill of joy. Their poverty had been hard, and the waiting and disappointments; but even if the Homestake Mine turned out to be a world-beater she would always feel that somehow it was *his*. But when Wunpost came back he did not stop at the ranch—she saw him passing by on the trail.

He rode in hot haste, heading grimly for Blackwater, and when he spurred down the main street the crowd set up a yell, for they had learned to watch for him now. When Wunpost came to town there was sure to be something doing, something big that called for the drinks; and all the pocket-miners and saloon bums were there, lined up to see him come in. But whether he had made a strike in his lucky way or was back for another bout with Eells was more than any man could say.

"Hello, there!" hailed a friend, or pseudo-friend, stepping out to make him stop at the saloon, "hold on, what's biting you now?"

"Can't stop," announced Wunpost, spurring on towards the bank, "by grab, I've had a bad dream!"

"A dream, eh?" echoed the friend, and then the crowd laughed and followed on up to the bank. Since Wunpost had lost in his bet with Eells and deposited all his money in the bank he was looked upon almost with pride as a picturesque asset of the town. He made talk, and that was made into publicity, and publicity helped the town. And now this mad prank upon which he seemed bent gave promise of even greater renown. So he had had a bad dream? That piqued their curiosity, but they were not kept long in doubt. Dismounting at the bank, he glanced up at the front and then made a plunge through the bank.

"Gimme my money!" he demanded, bringing his fist down with a bang and making a grab for a check. "Gimme all of it—every danged cent!"

He started to write and threw the pen to the floor as it sputtered and ruined his handiwork.

"Why, what's the matter, Mr. Calhoun?" cried Eells in astonishment, as the crowd came piling in.

"Gimme a pen!" commanded Wunpost, and, having seized the cashier's, he began laboriously to write. "There!" he said, shoving the check through the wicket; and then he stood waiting, expectant.

The cashier glanced at the check and passed it back to Eells, who had hastened behind the grille, and then they looked at each other in alarm.

"Why—er—this check," began Eells, "calls for forty-two thousand, eight hundred and fifty-two dollars. Do you want all that money now?"

"W'y, sure!" shrilled Wunpost, "didn't I tell you I wanted it?"

"Well, it's rather unusual," went on Judson Eells lamely, and then he spoke in an aside to his cashier.

"No! None of that, now!" burst out Wunpost in a fury, "don't you frame up any monkey-business on me! I want my money, see? And I want it right now! Dig up, or I'll wreck the whole dump!"

He brought his hand down again and Judson Eells retired while the cashier began to count out the bills.

"Here!" objected Wunpost, "I don't want all that small stuff—where's those thousand dollar bills I turned in? They're *gone?* Well, for cripes' sake, did you think they were a *present?*"

The clerk started to explain, but Wunpost would not listen to him.

"You're a bunch of crooks!" he burst out indignantly. "I only deposited that money on a bet! And here you turn loose and spend the whole roll, and start to pay me back in fives and tens."

"No, but Mr. Calhoun," broke in Judson Eells impatiently, "you don't understand how banking is done."

"Yes I do!" yelled back Wunpost, "but, by grab, I had a dream, and I dreamt that your danged bank was *broke!* Now gimme my money, and give it to me quick or I'll come in there and git it myself!"

He waited, grim and watchful, and they counted out the bills while he nodded and stuffed them into his shirt. And then they brought out gold in government-stamped sacks and he dropped them between his feet. But the gold was

295

not enough, and while Eells stood pale and silent the clerk dragged out the silver from the vault. Wunpost took them one by one, the great thousand dollar sacks, and added them to the pile at his feet, and still his demand was unsatisfied.

"Well, I'm sorry," said Eells, "but that's all we have. And I consider this very unfair."

"Unfair!" yelled Wunpost. "W'y, you doggone thief, you've robbed me of two thousand dollars. But that's all right," he added; "it shows my dream was true. And now your tin bank *is* broke!"

He turned to the crowd, which looked on in stunned silence, and tucked in his money-stuffed shirt.

"So I'm a blow-hard, am I?" he inquired sarcastically, and no one said a word.

CHAPTER XXIX

IN TRUST

THERE was cursing and wailing and gnashing of teeth in Blackwater's saloons that night, and some were for hanging Wunpost; but in the morning, when they woke up and found Eells and Lapham gone, they transferred their rage to them. A committee composed of the dummy directors, who had allowed Eells to do what he would, discovered from the books that the bank had been looted and that Eells was a fugitive from justice. He had diverted the bank's funds to his own private uses, leaving only his unsecured notes; and Lapham, the shrewd fox, had levied blackmail on his chief by charging huge sums for legal service. And now they were both gone and the Blackwater depositors had been left without a cent.

It was galling to their pride to see Wunpost stalking about and exhibiting his dream-restored wealth; but no one could say that he had not warned them, and he was loser by two thousand dollars himself. But even at that they considered it poor taste when he hung a piece of crepe on the door. As for the God-given dream which he professed to have received, there were those who questioned its authenticity; but whatever his hunch was, it had saved him forty-odd thousand dollars, which he had deposited with Wells Fargo and Company. They had never gone broke yet, as far as he knew, and they had started as a Pony Express.

But there was one painful feature about his bank-wrecking triumph which Wunpost had failed to anticipate, and as poor people who had lost their all came and stood before the bank he hung his head and moved on. It was all right for Old Whiskers and men of his stripe, whose profession was predatory itself; but when the hard-rock miners and road-makers came in the heady wine of triumph lost its bead. There are no palms of victory without the dust of vain regrets to mar their gleaming leaves, and when he saw Wilhelmina riding in from Jail Canyon he retreated to a doorway and winced. This was to have been his high spot, his magnum of victory; but somehow he sensed that no great joy would come from it, although of course she had it coming to her. And Wilhelmina simply stared at the sign "Bank Closed" and leaned against the door and cried.

That was too much for Wunpost, who had been handing out five dollars to all of the workingmen who were broke, and he strode across the street and approached her.

"What *you* crying about?" he asked, and when she shook her head he shuffled his feet and stood silent. "Come on up to the office," he said at last, and she followed him to the bare little room. There a short time before he had interceded to save her when she had all but signed the contract with Eells; but now at one blow he had destroyed what was built up and left her without a cent.

"What you crying about?" he repeated, as she sank down by the desk and fixed him with her sad, reproachful eyes, "you ought to be tickled to death."

"Because I've lost all my money," she answered dejectedly, "and we owe the contractors for the road."

"Oh, that's all right," he said, "I'll get you some more money. But say, didn't you do what I said? Why, I told you the last thing before I went away to git that first payment money *out!*"

"You did not!" she denied, "you told me to draw a few hundred. And then you turned around and deposited all you had, so I thought the bank must be safe."

"What—safe with Judson Eells? Safe with Lapham behind the scenes? Say, you'll never do at all. Have you heard the big news? Well, they've both skipped to Mexico and the depositors won't get a cent."

"Then what about my contract?" she burst out tearfully, "I've sold him my mine and now he's run away, so who's going to make the next payment?"

"They ain't nobody," grinned Wunpost, "and that's just the point—I told you I'd come back with his scalp!"

"Yes, but what about *us?*" she clamored accusingly, "who's going to pay for the road and all? Oh, I knew all the time that you'd never forgive me, and now you've just ruined everything."

"Never asked me to forgive you," defended Wunpost stoutly, "but I don't mind admitting I was sore. It's all right, of course, if you think you can play the game—but I never thought you'd rob a *friend!*"

"But you dared me to!" she cried, "and didn't I offer it for almost nothing, just to keep you from getting killed? And then, after I'd done everything to get back your contract you didn't even say 'Thanks!'"

"No, sure not," he agreed, "what should I be thanking *you* for? Did I ask you to get back my grubstake? Not by a long shot I didn't—what I wanted was my mine, and you turned around and sold it to Eells. Well, where's your friend now, and his yeller dog, Lapham? Skally-hooting across the desert for Mexico!"

"And isn't my contract any good? Won't the bank take it, or anybody? Oh, I think you're just—just hateful!"

"You bet I am, kid!" he announced with a swagger, "that's my long suit, savvy—hate! I

300

never forgive an enemy and I never forget a friend, and the man don't live that can *do* me! I'll git him, if it takes a thousand years!"

"Oh, there you go," she sighed, dusting her desk off petulantly, and then she bowed her head in thought. "But I must say," she admitted, "you have done what you said. But I thought you were just bragging at the time."

"They *all* did!" he beamed, "but I've showed 'em, by grab—they ain't calling me a blow-hard now. These Blackwater stiffs that wanted to run me out of town are coming around now to borrow five. They took up with a crook, just because he boosted for their town, and now they're left holding the sack. But if they'd listened to me they wouldn't be left flat, because I told 'em I was after his hide. And say, you should've seen him, when I came into his bank and shoved that big check under his nose! He knowed what I was thinking and he never said: 'Boo!' I showed him whether I knew how to write!"

He laid back and grinned broadly and Wilhelmina smiled, though a wistful look had crept into her eyes.

"Then I suppose," she said, "you're always going to hate *me,* because of course I did steal your mine. But now I'm glad it's gone, because I wasn't happy a minute—do you think you can forgive me, sometime?"

301

She glanced up appealingly but his brows had come down and he was staring at her fiercely.

"Gone!" he roared, "your mine ain't gone! Ain't you ever read that contract we framed up? Well, the mine reverts to you the first time a payment isn't made or *if the buyer becomes a fugitive from justice!* Yeh, my friend slipped that in along with the rest of it, about death or an Act of God. Say, that's what you might call head work!"

He jerked his chin and grinned admiringly but Wilhelmina did not respond.

"Yes," she objected, "but how do I get the money to pay the men for building the road? Because the twenty-five thousand dollars that I had in the bank—"

"Get it?" cried Wunpost, "why you go up to your mine and dig out some big chunks of gold, and then you send it out and sell it at the mint and start a little bank of your own. But say, kid, you're all right—I like you and all that—but something tells me you ain't cut out for business. Now you'd better just turn this mine over to me—"

"Oh, *will* you take it back?" she cried out impulsively, leaping up and beginning to smile. "I've just *wanted* to give it to you but—well, of course I did steal it. And will you take me back for a friend?"

"Well, I might," conceded Wunpost, rising

302

slowly to his feet, and then he shook his head. "But you're no business woman," he stated, "what I was trying to say was—"

"Well, let's own it together!" she dimpled impatiently, and Wunpost accepted the trust.

Center Point Large Print
600 Brooks Road / PO Box 1
Thorndike ME 04986-0001 USA

(207) 568-3717

US & Canada:
1 800 929-9108
www.centerpointlargeprint.com

Coolidge, Dane, 1873-1940.
Wunpost [text (large print)]

JUL   2012